Leaving Beirut

Mai Ghoussoub

Leaving Beirut

Women and the Wars Within

Saqi Books

British Library Cataloguing-in-Publication Data
A catalogue record for this book is available from the
British Library

ISBN 0 86356 090 3 (pbk)

This edition first published 1998

Saqi Books
26 Westbourne Grove
London W2 5RH

Contents

A Kind of Madness

The laws of the State were flouted, no tradition,
no moral code was respected ... In the collapse of
all values a kind of madness gained hold.
Stefan Zweig

The phone had only rung twice when she picked up the receiver. She thought she would never get used to the indifference with which the phone was treated in Paris. She herself had often hung up when she had made a call and nobody had answered at the other end by the third or fourth ring. People here didn't feel the urge to jump to the phone as soon as it started ringing. Maybe it was because their homes were less crowded and less likely to have somebody always sitting next to the handset. As soon as she lifted the receiver she knew, from the slight, familiar disturbance on the line, that the call was from Lebanon.

'Beirut calling, hold the line.' The voice of a bored female phone operator in Beirut.

Her heart sank. She could never help feeling nervous when she was connected to Beirut, and she reacted resentfully towards her irrational agitation. Whenever she was drawn back into the country she had left, she was no longer in full control and her pulse would run at a fast pace. Faster than she wished. Impatiently, irritatedly, she waited to be connected.

'Go ahead love, you have Paris,' said the same off-hand voice to whoever was calling from the other end. It was him. It was the same voice that she believed she had silenced forever in her ears. This voice did not belong here. It should have stayed where it had been left, muzzled under the rubble of the collapsing buildings of Beirut, safely confined behind the austere scrutiny of the immigration authorities. It had no right intruding into her new universe, her cosy Parisian exile. This voice, his voice, was a transgression, a trespasser into her acquired space. She hung up in the middle of his desperate hellos. 'Can you hear me . . .? Hello . . . Hello . . .' She hung up violently. Angry with him, yes with him, only him. He had no business invading her new serenity. He belonged to a war that she had escaped and that she never wanted to be reminded of again.

The phone rang again. She rushed to unplug it. The sound of silence in the room was deep and devastating. She turned her back on the table where the lifeless telephone stood, and moved towards the window. She tried to immerse herself in the enchanted sight of reclining roofs competing for space on the city's horizon. She had been lucky to find this flat. Here, on the top floor of this old building, at the end of a winding, narrow street. L'Impasse des Eaux Douces, in the heart of the Latin Quarter, she had spent hours observing the angles created by all these cluttered roofs, imagining the lives that unfolded beneath them. This was her present panorama, one that she had made and designed for herself. A tangible reality, with a starting point that she had drawn as an act of will, reducing her past and taming its recollections. His voice, his existence must not interfere with this landscape . . . She will not allow it . . . she cannot afford to . . .

Allen came from behind her and put his hands on her shoulders. She jumped. 'What is it darling? Sorry, didn't you hear me coming? Who was that on the phone?'

'No one. I unplugged the phone. I don't want to talk about it.'

Allen's face could not hide emotion. She had been attracted to the serenity of his eyes, to his cool and nonchalant manner. She had met him in the English bookshop one Saturday afternoon a few months previously, and now he stayed with her when he came to Paris. He came regularly, every other weekend and during the academic holidays. She appreciated his discretion and valued his easy-going attitude. She was always grateful to him for not insisting on explanations. Yet somehow at that instant his controlled performance seemed theatrical. It was irritating. It had the smell of inhibition and had lost its charm. She moved away from him abruptly, took her jacket and walked out of the flat. She went swiftly down the steps, avoiding Madame Dufour's cat and ignoring the scrutiny of its piercing green eyes. She walked firmly out of the building, giving the concierge no chance to step out of her cubbyhole and engage her in one of her tedious conversations.

She walked tensely and hastily. The walk of a harassed woman. A woman distressed by the persistent resurfacing of her past, suddenly reaching into the present. She had no space left in her heart for the nagging guilt triggered by Allen's sad expression. Her blunt rejection of his kindness was the best she could manage. She needed to empty her heart totally in order to be able to survive. She had already once previously gathered all the cruelty she could muster in order to dump the voice that had reappeared in her life today. She had somehow believed that the man whose desperate voice she'd heard on the phone was locked away in the city she had abandoned, relegated to an epoch that was past and gone.

For the first time since moving into her Parisian flat she walked through the familiar streets of her *quartier* oblivious to the colours and joys of the busy vegetable market, insensitive to the temptations of its shop windows, and unaware of an invigorating breeze announcing an early Spring. She did not stop at her *café-bistrot* for the sweet, lazy ritual of sipping an espresso while watching the passers-by. She could not bear the idea of staying still. She needed to keep on moving. Walking stubbornly ahead. Trying to stop her thoughts from drifting back to the place where his voice had come from, to the amputated memories of a torn city that had once been hers.

Beirut exhaled a fragrance of damp earth. A sweet, teasing scent filled her nostrils. A triumphant sun had cleared the grey thickness from the sky, appeasing its anger with an offering of blue. The fear of death that had emptied the streets and left them grieving seemed to have faded away as if by a miracle. Her body felt powerful and she stepped forward cheerfully. The Palestinian camp of Sabra was waking into life. A smell of dark tea emanated from precarious shacks, seeping through the hesitant openings of their narrow doorways. Children rushed impetuously in the narrow alleys, and their mothers poured water onto concrete floors and then swept it out of their clustering homes with a generous thrust. The camp, usually so noisy and busy, was still testing the vulnerable silence that follows the rage and roar of combat. Inside the medical centre where she was heading, the walls were an immaculate white, and voices were hushed. But the discreet manners of the staff were not sufficient to cushion their patients from the world outside. How could anyone hope to separate the 'inside' from the 'outside' in a place where the roof was made of corrugated tin and the front door opened immediately onto the clamour of the alley and the invading dust of its unpaved earth? She wondered this every time she stepped into the 'hospital', as the people of the camp liked to call it. She was working here, helping to classify the medicines on the shelves and translating their instructions into Arabic. She had been coming here once a week since the beginning of the war, and it was here for the first time that her involvement with the Leftist movement had felt meaningful and concrete. Here, among the angry complaints and the patient resignation of the wounded, next to a chaotic group of women carrying sick children and attempting to pacify the healthy ones they had brought with them, she realised the extent of her abhorrence of her own class – the middle class – with its paranoid fear of these people, and their lack of compassion for the 'unhygienic camps' into which none of them had ever set foot.

She looked alien in the camp, and this bothered her. The way she dressed was out of tune with the long, ample skirts worn by the camp's women, or the headscarves that modestly covered their hair. She could never bring herself to play at looking 'genuine', exchanging her jeans for a long dress just before entering the camp to fulfil her militant duties, as some of her female comrades did. She would have thought this theatrical, and she had no time for what she regarded as 'populist hypocrisy'. She walked through the muddy alleys with the slightly hurried pace of an apparently confident woman.

The air of agitation at the medical centre was explained by the presence of two open-top Jeeps squeezed into the alley next door. She had to advance sideways in order to reach the door and step inside. He stopped speaking and his eyes moved towards the door where she was standing. The two nurses and the doctor were sitting in front of him and she could hardly see them. There was a thicket of armed men standing around in the reception area, drastically reducing its size, and thickening the air with a fug of Marlboro cigarettes. A few awkward seconds passed, heavy with embarrassing silence, before the doctor introduced her and invited her to sit down.

Abu Firas was not as tall as she had imagined. He had been much talked of since the war began. She avoided looking at him, for fear of betraying her inner agitation and her intense curiosity. He had a reputation as a tough leader, a dangerous warrior and a secretive manipulator. She knew he was watching her while he questioned the medical staff about their needs and the problems the clinic was facing in those troubled times. The men went on drawing deeply on their cigarettes, adjusting the Kalashnikovs on their shoulders and listening silently with the deep concentration of chain-smokers. He, for his part, held his cigarette between his thumb and index finger – a nervous, bony hand, from which a deep heat seemed to emanate.

She was incapable of following the conversation, and was powerless to stop herself staring at his hands, with their angular, forceful impact. The haze that enveloped the smoky room had blurred her vision and her sense of reality. She was taken by surprise when she realised that he was already saying goodbye and preparing to leave, followed by his fighters and guards who were now vigorous and alert. When she could no longer hear the squealing tyres of the departing cars, she moved towards the shelves that she had come to organize. Her movements and her thoughts were slower than she intended; the vision of his dark, penetrating eyes and the movement of his warm, agile hands lingered persistently in her mind's eye. It suddenly occurred to her that, unlike most Arab men, he had no moustache. This fact amused her. She caught herself smiling. An hour or so later, with the medicines on the shelf still far from organized, she heard a vehicle screech to a halt in the alley outside the clinic. One of Abu Firas's bodyguards stepped abruptly into the room, sucking on his Marlboro and utterly unimpressed by the sign on the door announcing 'Please knock before entering'.

'Abu Firas asked me to take you to his office. There's something urgent that he needs to discuss with you. I will drive you there.' She knew that she should have shown hesitation, or maybe said something about needing to finish her work, but she was incapable of resisting her desire to follow him. She picked up the navy-blue jacket that she wore while about her militant duties, but as she put it on she wished that she had not tried so hard to look shapeless and unkempt.

She found it hard to recall how she had come into his office or how she had climbed the stairs of the building where the bodyguard had taken her. She wasn't really listening to Abu Firas's long and serious-sounding speech about how much the revolution needed people like her. His phrases didn't seem to be made of words. Their messages were lost in her desire to be closer to his hands, to be warmed by the heat that emanated from their tense movements. She was pleasantly taken aback when he told his bodyguard that he no longer needed him. The voice of the bodyguard saying goodbye sounded curiously incorporeal. She heard the sound of the door closing, and unknowingly she moved towards those hands and towards him.

This was the beginning of a passion that was immersed in war and danger, fired by its secrecy and its proximity to death and destruction. She had plunged into an adventure of perilous abnormality, knowing its dangers but doing nothing to resist them.

She had reached the Place du Châtelet, having walked down Boulevard St Michel without having realised it. The openness of the pedestrianized square and its lively comings and goings irritated her and drew her back into the present. Why was she walking so fast . . . behaving like a woman on the run . . . a fugitive? Beirut was far away. She had choices. She could step inside the Théâtre de la Ville, or walk back towards the bridge. She could abandon herself to the soft flow of the Seine and allow its comforting presence to calm her. She didn't have to dash about like this. She could push back the memories and assign a more recent starting-point to her personal history, perpetuating what she had achieved before the damned telephone call of that afternoon. What she had done in Beirut, and the way she had behaved there, was none of her responsibility. It had happened in the midst of a generalised dementia. Now she lived here, beside a great, glittering river, in a great and vivacious city, light years away from the morbidity that she had witnessed during that aberrant period of her life.

But those three rings of the phone had been enough to take all the serenity away from her, to bring back strange and unfathomable feelings of guilt, and an uncertainty that was now making her rush about on city pavements, faster than Paris was used to.

'The responsibility is mine too. I was blinded by passion and lost my lucidity. I fooled myself that I was joining a revolution, one that would stop misery and injustice. But I used him. I used him to belong. To harvest energy from the fear of death that was spreading around. I suppressed the fear in my body beneath the warmth of his embrace. There was the night when I could not let go of his body and kept drawing him back into me with the rhythm of the shelling that was pounding relentlessly, violently shaking the building where we met in secret. I gladly repressed questions about the meaning of what was happening, about its contradiction with the ideals we had all started from. I kept moving and doing things instead of stopping and questioning. I lost any sense of normality and called on his body to take me deeper into the dizziness of the unknown ...'

She must have been talking to herself. People were giving her embarrassed looks. She was speaking out loud as if to hear for herself what she had not been willing to tell anyone else.

Allen's discretion had been tactful, but she wished he had been more forceful, less respectful of the years before he met her. Maybe then she wouldn't have ended up like a crazy woman talking to herself on the pavements of Paris. By now she was on the Rue du Rivoli, approaching the Louvre, and the streets were full of tourists. She felt more sympathetic to them at that moment, now that she suddenly saw herself as a visitor in Paris rather than a person whose life had begun here, only a few months ago, at the gates of Orly airport.

She turned right at the Palais Royal and looked for a cafe where she could rest her feet and calm her anguished mind over an espresso. She needed to be in control. She knew that she could no longer escape the intrusion of her own story. She ordered a bottle of mineral water and a coffee, and felt an urge to smoke a cigarette, as if the act of smoking, which she had given up, might seal her decision to take a look backwards. She looked in her pocket and found an old electric bill and a Bic pen that was broken at one end. The waiter was tidying up for the end of his shift, and she settled the bill promptly, eager to be left alone with her thoughts and the blank space on the back of the electric bill.

Dear Abu Firas,

So it was you on the phone today! I apologize for having hung up on you. I could not face hearing your voice. Just as I am not able to face the woman that I was when I was near you. I know you suffered a lot when I disappeared. I can still see the despair in your eyes as you looked into my sudden coldness and my inexplicable metamorphosis during our last meeting. You were speechless. The woman who had longed for your caresses, whose desires seemed never satiated, was turning her back on you, refusing to grant even the hint of an explanation. This woman was at a loss with her own transformation and could not offer a justification that did not exist.

You see, when my brother was wounded, you insisted on coming to the hospital to be near me and help console my parents. But my brother's wounds and the despair of my parents had thrust me back into my previous world, one in which the war and the tragic condition of those who suffered it, was as real as burning flesh. The shattered faces anxiously waiting in the hospital corridors stripped away the abstractness of the war. It was no longer possible to hear the war as an exaltation of detonating sounds, or see it as a constellation of strangely beautiful night-lit skies. Nor could it be justified by wishful thinking and self-gratifying beliefs. The slogans that we had advanced blew up in my face. My passion for you retracted from my body, leaving a dreadful aftertaste; my thoughts were troubled as if blurred by the ache of an instantaneous hangover. My brother's pain suddenly exposed all the wounds I had chosen not to see in the months we had been together. The anguished faces of the wives, the friends and the relatives of those pain-tormented patients squeezed together in the crowded hospital corridors became unbearable witnesses to my own carelessness. You should not have come into those corridors, into the reality of my family. You should not have become real. We could only belong in abnormality; we were only real inside an actuality that was aberrant; we made love frantically and grew more passionate only because of it.

I have not forgotten my excitement on that night when I realised that one of your visitors was an international smuggler. He spoke of the leaders of the other camp, your 'enemies', with great familiarity. I tried to listen to the conversation through the closed door. I felt no need to judge this man then. You, on the other hand, didn't want me mixing with him. I recall you telling me after he left: 'The road to liberation cannot be pure and clean.' You didn't like him. I wanted to join you in the room with him but you wouldn't allow me. My excitement was like that of a teenager meeting an actor from a film she has just seen. I had heard of these smugglers who had no friend and no cause and who traded with both sides, and I was curious to see one in the flesh. For me it was a game. Like entering a forbidden world. For you, it was a dirty business you had to go through, and one where you did not want me involved.

I left the country as soon as my brother's life was out of danger. I never looked back. I started hating all those who held a weapon in the name of a cause. I grew intolerant of their rationalisations. I thought that by obliterating the past I could erase my own involvement. I would be able to say to myself, 'I never held a weapon, I was just trying to help those whom my society was oppressing. I closed my eyes to the cruelties, the orgy of retaliation and reaction that spread around me.' I didn't want to look at the crimes that were being perpetrated by the men I was mixing with, some of whom are called martyrs today. I drowned my anguish in the thrills of lustful indulgence. I could not have explained this to you then, for I did not understand it myself at the time. I cultivated amnesia, because it was easier that way. I built a world with no past in it. But it took just one telephone call to prove how fragile and artificial my creation had been.

I was lucky. I had the possibility of leaving. Many were stuck in the war and didn't have the luxury of avoiding involvement in it. But the bliss of amnesia seems to be short-lived, and the desire to ignore my own responsibilities was a flimsy subterfuge against guilt. The most difficult thing for me to acknowledge is that I blinded myself deliberately for such a long time. It took the ripped and torn body of my brother to release me. What right do I have now to blame those who continued indulging in the abnormality of war?

I attempted a total transmutation. I had to move into a brand new setting, come to foreign lands and hear a different language before I could realise how terrible and absurd this whole thing had been. I needed to cross thousands of miles to see what it was like to live once again outside this orgy of violence and death, and to realise how terribly cruel our cruelty was.

By now she was writing over the bill itself. She hadn't noticed the blue ink staining her fingers from the broken Bic. She knew she would never send the letter, but she needed to keep on writing. A new waiter was setting the tables around her for dinner. He gave her a quick smile and she wondered if it meant that he wanted her to move, or that he didn't intend to disturb her. More lights were switched on in the cafe, and she looked outside. The cheerful luminosity of the sky had gone, plunging the day into a rosy-blue melancholy. A group of five or six teenagers made a boisterous entrance into the cafe. They were speaking loudly, boastfully, jostling with youthful energy. She glanced rapidly at her table before leaving, as if to be sure that no trace of her secret remained on its surface. She walked out slowly, embracing the rhythms of Paris as darkness settled. She began to head for home. She was happy to face the night. The road between the Palais Royal and her apartment in the Latin Quarter felt like a peaceful interlude, a serene pause between her troubled memories and a future that was vague.

Allen did not question her when she returned to the flat and plugged the phone back in. He did not even ask where she had been or how she was feeling. He was preparing dinner and flicking through a book he had brought with him. A hardback on Feyerabend's theory of knowledge which he would tell her about enthusiastically during dinner. Would she have opened up to him if he had been more insistent? He noted teasingly that she had drunk more than her usual portion of their *vin de table*. His lovely English accent, with its tendency to stretch and tilt the 'in' in *vin* and open up the 'a' in *table*, was a pleasant reminder of their first encounter. His calm poise put her at ease, and having hastily cleared the table she settled in front of her desk. She was eager to wander back through her memories, and she wanted to write.

You too were a nicer man than the man the war turned you into. I could feel your sudden yearning for gentleness, and your need to confide in the woman who was making love to you. But the woman who I was then rejected all your efforts to humanize the relationship. That woman was indulging in a voluptuous alienation of her body from her senses and feelings. Nothing around me really made sense, and I did not want you to be real and human in the midst of all the confusion. The closeness of those combative males in whose circles you moved threw me into cycles of rejection and attraction that were only appeased by your embrace. Even then I loathed this excess of maleness that had taken hold of my city, but I dismissed my feelings in the sheltering warmth of your hands. I escaped my fears by endlessly testing my vulnerability. I suppressed them by walking into dangers, and you kept being amazed at what you thought was my courage. I did not speak much to you. I only cared for the suffering of the others, all the others, of what I called 'humanity'. Yet I denied the humanity of the man who was the closest to me, and whom I so often drew passionately inside me. My passion was just a symptom of the war. I could never explain this to you, and when I walked out of the war I erased your existence like those soldiers who prefer to leave their shame buried in the lands to which they have been sent to fight.

What tortures me now is the haunting question of how I would have behaved if I were still in the demonic grip of the killing and cruelty that had possessed my country. Would I have been able to keep on shutting my eyes and evading the absurdity of it all by disappearing into my body and reducing myself to it? Would my reason have been swept entirely away by this whirlpool of barbarism and savagery?

'Why is the West so enraged about one kidnapped man, when in our country we all live like prisoners in a war zone?' If I had

stayed, would I have said terrible things like that? Maybe I was afraid of speaking to you because I was afraid of what I might have turned into if I had stayed in Beirut. Maybe if I heard you talk, I would not have felt free to condemn all the cruelty that I see and observe from a distance? Maybe I am just afraid of sharing the responsibility.

That night she went to sleep without her usual fear of the night and its nightmares. And that night she dreamt of Mrs Nomy.

Mrs Nomy's Lesson

I must have been about 12 years old. Madame Nomy looked old to me then. I suppose she must have been in her early thirties. She was a short lady, fair-haired, and she always dressed in a dignified sober suit. She taught us French at the *Lycée Français de Jeunes Filles*. This meant that she was the most important teacher, for the French teacher also taught French history, French geography and science. Mrs Nomy was what we called *une maîtresse sevère* and I took her very seriously. I actually wanted to impress her. I still wonder whether Mrs Nomy took me equally seriously on that day when she told me to come and stand next to her desk, and handed me my essay, for which she had given me a grade of 10 (out of 20). I was one of her best students, and this was the first time I had received anything under 14 for an essay. Standing there, facing her, with my profile to the other 25 or so students, I felt both vulnerable and angry. I thought I had done an essay that was very good, one that had been aimed specifically at pleasing and impressing our diminutive but imposing teacher. I recall very well the topic that she had given us the previous week: 'Describe in four pages an event that has deeply affected you in your life.'

We were given an hour to write it, and it never occurred to

me to write the truth. All I wanted was to do well, very well. I prepared myself to use the most sophisticated vocabulary I could manage, the best composition of text I could construct, and to get as close as possible to a particular poem by Victor Hugo – *La Conscience* – that Mrs Nomy seemed to like so much. I asked myself what was the gist of the poem. A wide-open eye followed Cain wherever he went. However deep his hiding place, the eye was there, staring at him. Cain was not to go unpunished after killing his brother. Even if no other human being or authority was calling for his punishment, his own conscience demanded revenge. He would not get away with his crime. The eye of blame was always there, following him to the darkest and most unreachable of places. In the end he dug a tomb, in which he hoped to bury himself and escape the eye. But 'the eye was in the tomb watching Cain'.

That was it. The theme of my essay would be the power of revenge, and its merits. So I concocted a pretty stupid little story which, at the time, seemed marvellous to me. I should repeat it here, for the sake of what will follow. I wrote a little 'confession' about 'last summer' when five of my playmates played a nasty trick on me. They had organized a walk, in the late evening, to the little forest where we used to play every afternoon next to our summer house in the mountains. Once inside the forest, we started playing hide and seek, and suddenly they all disappeared. I looked around and found myself alone. I waited for what seemed to me an eternity, becoming more and more anxious as the sky got darker and the sound of the rustling leaves and shivering branches sharper. I was starting to shiver and cry when suddenly five ghosts, all dressed in white, came and surrounded me, shouting 'Whoo-Whoo' as they flapped their white sheets in my face.

I remember that in my story I had written about falling on the floor, hiding my face and crying my heart out. That was when my playmates took off the white sheets that covered them from head to toe and began laughing at my fear, my misery and my shame. It was at that point that I intended to use the Hugo poem that my teacher loved. I thought my vocabulary would impress her. I wrote: 'I looked at the other children with a *regard foudroyant*, staring deeply with all the intensity of my choleric frustration at the dark sky and its sparkling stars, and pledged to the stars and planets that soon, very soon, I would take my REVENGE. The insult I had suffered would be paid for dearly, and JUSTICE WOULD BE DONE.'

I was expecting a 16 or even the very rare grade of 18, for I had used all the themes that had seemed to be important to Mrs Nomy during the final weeks of that academic year. Even her insistence that the cosmos was made of many planets had found a place in my four pages. But here was Mrs Nomy, with her eyes looking even smaller than usual, holding my dissertation and telling me in an accusing tone '*Je vous ai donné 10 sur 20, bien plus que vous ne meritez.*' She used the same tone to tell me how disgusting it was to harbour bitter feelings towards one's friends. And that even if their joke had been a bit malicious, I should have had a bigger heart and been more generous towards my fellow human beings. Revenge, she said, was the meanest of human sentiments, the most cowardly way one could behave. Even if my vocabulary had been rich, she said, it was despicable, because it described base sentiments.

'That is why you deserve far less than the grade I gave you, but I am a teacher and I cannot give you a grade that will affect your general average. The composition of the text is technically competent and there are hardly any spelling mistakes. Go back to your seat. I am disappointed in you.'

It took me a very long time to get to sleep that night. I was confused and puzzled. I had constructed a story that suited the vocabulary I intended to display, and I had borrowed an idea from a great poet whom my teacher admired. I might have gone to Mrs Nomy and disclosed these facts, but then she might have accused me of plagiarism and insincerity. At the same time, I found that I agreed with her. I admired her so much that I kept repeating the words she had said. I wanted to go straight back to her, to assure her that I had no place for revenge in my heart and that I would always enlarge my soul to make space for generosity in it. In the end I fell asleep, and when I went into class the following day, Mrs Nomy went about her routine as if nothing had happened. I understood that I was expected to do the same.

Did Mrs Nomy realise the immeasurable effect that her little speech had had on me? I don't mean just then, but still even now. Most probably not. Children have a tendency to inflate the little remarks that adults make, even when they're said without thinking. A few years later, in 1967, there was no more Mrs Nomy to be seen, walking with her fast little steps through the school courtyard. We believed what some of the older students were whispering: that Mrs Nomy had run away to Israel, that she was Jewish, and that she didn't feel safe here any more.

It had somehow occurred to me at the time that Mrs Nomy was not just speaking lightly to one of her *jeunes filles* when she had castigated me for my vengeful intentions. Quite the opposite. Mrs Nomy was speaking as an adult who knew exactly what she meant. She was trying to help us to understand people's complex reactions to survival, and the difficulties of salvaging kindness in the harsh reality of this Middle East where people both live and condemn each other to exile. She had chosen the way of forgiveness, and was trying to teach it to her students.

An Uneasy Peace

Wherever you are today, Mrs Nomy, I wish you could hear me now. I want to thank you for the lasting influence that you have exercised over us, your *jeunes filles* of so many years ago. Most of all, I wish you could have been with me in Beirut last month, when I returned after a long time spent out of the city because of the civil war.

Beirut is living its peace now. Like all the others who are returning here, and those who still live here, I wanted to believe in this peace. I wanted to enjoy it to the full, to scream enthusiastically at the sight of a new restaurant, a new shop window, 'you see!'. The Beirutis who *stayed* (there is a post-war Lebanese vocabulary that divides those who left from those who stayed; I imagine it must be similar in all cities that have known disasters and big waves of emigration) would say 'We have very fancy things now. Have you seen that beautiful new restaurant they've just opened in Verdun Street?' They leave the second part of their sentence unuttered: 'It easily matches your best restaurants in Europe.' And I, like a happy parrot, would make a big thing of this new restaurant, as the proof, the absolute confirmation, that the war had ended.

But whenever I had a minute to myself, I felt a strange

malaise taking hold of me. My initial solution was never to be alone, never to give myself time to face my thoughts. Run for your peace of mind – keep running to other people, and stay with them. Until one cool afternoon when, for some inexplicable reason, I suddenly stopped running. The sun was shy but friendly. I was standing on my parents' balcony – a situation that I had often dreamt of in London, when the sky had been low and grey and the rain slow and steady. Maybe because I was tired, or maybe because the view from the balcony had not changed since my childhood, I just stood still. I didn't do anything. I knew I had to face this nagging malaise. Why on earth couldn't I just go and enjoy this *paix retrouvée* without feeling guilty and uneasy about it?

Wasn't it bliss, that suddenly nobody seemed to retain a real grudge against 'the others' – those same others who two years previously had been the enemy who was ready to annihilate us? Nobody was calling for inquiries into this or that massacre. Wouldn't you have approved of this attitude, Mrs Nomy. 'Revenge is the meanest of sentiments.' Do you remember telling me that in front of all my classmates? Even people who had lost a son, a brother or a wife were not expressing blame towards the perpetrators. It was a conscious effort to start all over again – as if everything that had happened had been a terrible nightmare, and now that we were awake we should be trying to forget the ugly images of the night in order to step into a bright new day. Even the black humour of war gave way to talk about the crazy prices – 'everything is so expensive' – or to packed vaudeville shows at the theatre.

I used to join in with the cynical remarks of friends playing at looking smart and sophisticated and half mocking the Lebanese people's own description of themselves: 'The Lebanese. They are tough survivors ... They appreciate good living ... They dress elegantly as they extract themselves from wars and misery.' Survivors? I guess that this survival was not a matter of choice for them or for anyone else. But as far as good living is concerned, yes, maybe there is some Mediterranean truth in that, and it is admirable in its way. But why this malaise? Why do I wish I could have Mrs Nomy next to me again, and ask her one more time to repeat the words 'forgive' and 'forget' until they become as reassuring and relaxing as the words of a hypnotist? Otherwise, how am I going to deal with the feelings of vulnerability that creep in every time I stop running? Can one forget and learn lessons for the future? Is there a way to forget – to live, laugh, make love, bring up new babies and create – without once having to ask: 'And why would it not start all over again?'.

Remember, we live on the shores of the Mediterranean. Honour, revenge and vendetta are virtues that our menfolk are supposed to have defended throughout their history. Have fifteen years of civil war had more influence than centuries of memory? Did the civil war do what our society has a habit of doing each time it faces a crisis: veil its women a little more and make it easier for its men to take risks? Or is it that there has been so much cruelty and madness that it makes no sense trying to extract lessons from it? When you've been in Europe and seen the TV and newspaper images of young people smiling and raising their arms in the fascist salute, after you've seen the bodies of victims of racist attacks and the shocked faces of their relatives, what can you say?

Tell me, Mrs Nomy, are the people in the country that you and I left behind wiser when they choose to opt for a touch of amnesia? Are they looking forward towards life and its future, or are they being shallow and irresponsible? Does anyone have a clear-cut answer to this? I recently read an article by the Lebanese novelist Hassan Daoud, entitled 'He is one of those who stayed'. The article was commenting on a French TV programme made in 1993, on life in Beirut after the war. He wrote:

'We looked as if we Lebanese had exchanged war for *tarab*, the sensual pleasure of music. In this programme they showed us preparing the material for our *tarab*, in the same way as we had previously prepared the materials necessary for the pursuit of war. The public watching the concerts is always an intrinsic part of the festival, for anarchy is the order of the day: some sit, some stand, some dance between the tables and the seats ... the audience does not differentiate between one singer and the next ... it is as if the artist is just a mouthpiece for the songs that are stored inside the audience.' Hassan recalls the crazy parties and singing sessions that were often held inside homes during the war: 'It was as if our fun at night could match the intensity of the violence that was occurring during the day.'

Hassan's words whisper back to me that there is more to the touch of amnesia that the Lebanese are cultivating so assiduously. Perhaps this fun after such a terrible war – in which nobody was a winner and in which everyone lost dearly and deeply – means that people are trying to push their lives ahead, to speed up the good moments, as if they are afraid to lose it all.

'This war follows us in our peace. Perhaps the French will say, as they watch us singing and dancing like this, that we look like a people going into war, not emerging from it.' Hassan concludes with these words: 'You don't see lone passers-by on the streets of Beirut at night, you don't see late-nighters on their own.'

The terrible thing about wars is that they turn individuals into mere members of groups, be they nations, gangs, militias, or some other kind of tribe. This may be why, when justice is done, it often looks absurd, for the criteria applied are those of a normal modern society, in which individuals are deemed responsible for their own actions. This is why, in an epoch where one's sense of justice abhors the tribal approach in which all are punishable as one and for one, no decent person can claim to be right in the punishments they are calling for. This was the dilemma of Hannah Arendt who, after pressure and passionate pleas from various quarters, agreed to edit and cut her courageous reporting of Eichmann's trial. This was also the genius of Ismail Kadare in writings such as *Broken April*, where he has us share the feelings and dilemmas of the individual whose emotions are in collision but are also inextricable from the demands of his society. His *Broken April* is a fresco of the sad fate of one human who is obliged to take revenge for his group even though he has no personal grudge against the person he is about to murder. This is perhaps why we sense a frustration seeping through the words of Hassan

Daoud, when he sees people still acting as groups and making as much loud, anarchic noise as did the bullets and artillery of the fighters in the times of war.

Here I am, standing silently on my Beirut balcony, puzzled and confused by my memories. And the unease remains. It is definitely not easy just to walk away and forget. Images of violence haunt me like the eye that haunted Cain. I identify with Cain. Like him, we were compelled to move from one country to another. Like the unwanted children of a happier humanity.

Masrah Farouk

My city had always been inclined to excess. Respectable people liked to refer to it as 'BBB' – brothels, banks and brawls. For myself, I felt secure amid these busy bees, always preferred to walk on busy 'indecent' pavements rather than through streets that were 'respectable' and deserted. In those days Beirut, rich or poor, muddy or lavishly paved, knew how to celebrate its nights. I loved walking through its late-night streets, I enjoyed both its flamboyant kitsch and its ritzy elegance. When its advertising hoardings still flashed, profligate in their use of electricity, and its drivers communicated with eager car-horns, you might have forgotten that the poor were still wretched after all. In those days Beirut exuded optimism and the most disadvantaged believed in its promises. In this bright, sparkling city, the poor had their little Edens. I once followed them in there. Masrah Farouk was the name of the place. A downtown, down-market little heaven.

How I happened to go there is a long story which I shall try to make short. I was flying back from a summer holiday in Paris. I was not yet nineteen. On the plane were the glamorous members of the French *Théâtre de la Comédie Française*, coming to perform in what was then the famous Baalbeck international festival. One of the actors wanted to visit authentic local cabarets. He had heard tell of Masrah Farouk, of its lost glamour and its decline. His girlfriend, a tall beauty with green, catlike eyes, wanted also to see the 'exotic sights' of Lebanon.

It took me a few days to convince some of my friends – who had grown up in the slums around Beirut, and who had built their way out of them through trade-union activities – to accompany us, the French couple and me, to this disreputable cabaret. My friends disliked the idea intensely. The cabaret was located in a narrow street off the Place des Martyrs, in a neighbourhood that 'any respectable woman should avoid after sunset'.

When they finally saw the looks of my French actress, they went mad. They gave me a dressing-down in Arabic. 'You want us to take this Marilyn Monroe into a place like that? We'll need weapons. You haven't seen the faces of the men who frequent your Masrah Farouk.'

My friends, it appeared, knew influential people in the milieu of downtown cabarets, and thanks to their acquaintances we had some 'protection' assigned to us. We were the only two women not on the stage at Masrah Farouk; the rest of the audience was all male and very much so. As we appeared through the door, some eighty to a hundred male faces, most with moustaches turned and looked in our direction. They were evidently puzzled by our presence, and stared in bewilderment at the blonde French-woman and her green eyes. They did not dare express their amazement in any other form, on account of the over-sized and nasty-looking men who had been allocated to protect us. 'Us', who were introduced to the management of the cabaret as 'representatives of the international art scene'. That was our alibi, our passport to seats that were used only to male posteriors. 'The world of high French art is visiting the arts scene of Beirut,' my Lebanese friend said loudly, looking at the rest of the audience with an over-wide smile. Our two protectors were not very discreet about being heavily armed, and stood behind us all through the show, the only two women in the place. I will never know whether the fact that we were accepted was due to toleration or to the Colt revolvers that our protectors revealed every time they stretched and adjusted their jackets.

The men in the seats around us were set for a great night, and their ebullient mood matched their expectations. Like us, they had paid two pounds apiece for a night of music, comedy and women entertainers. It was summer and it was hot. The barman, who carried his drinks in a box hanging from his shoulders by a broad black strap, walked up and down the theatre peering suspiciously at the clientèle and assessing the level of their thirst. His ferocious expression was the secret of his prosperity. He would arrive at your seat and automatically, even before consulting you, would open the bottle and announce the brand as if it was something you had just ordered. He chose the drinks he offered according to the faces of the customers. As he passed our seats he opened two bottles of 'imported' Fanta, his most expensive soft drink, handed them silently to us, and then waited quietly to be paid. None of the customers dared argue with him, for he had a thick, imposing moustache, and a sharp and visible knife attached to his belt.

People were there to be titillated, to forget about the misery of the day, or because it was nicer than sleeping in the shops where they worked all day. They weren't after fights or arguments. Not yet, anyway. Who needs to argue about the price of a cheap drink when the night is so full of promise?

Suddenly a thunderous sound erupted from behind the faded but none the less rich velvet curtain. The show was about to start, and a deep male voice introduced the first star of the evening: 'The Little Flower of Palestine'. We applauded energetically when a little ten-year-old girl, all dressed in white, began singing *'Ana Wardat Falastin'* – 'I am the flower of Palestine'. Her crystalline voice and childlike innocence were there to remind us that before the fun and spice we should remember the nationalist struggle. 'The little girl is going to bed now,' we were assured after she had left the stage. This fact was presumably revealed for the benefit of the 'Morality Police', who would anyway have been bribed to turn a blind eye.

Now the audience was ready for the whirling and shimmering of the belly dancer Farida: 'The Star of the East'. Farida advanced very slowly towards the stage. There were days when she could swirl like a serpent and shake like a glittering bubble. But today she was tired, and maybe a bit too fat, and her steps were those of swollen feet. Her shimmers consisted of bored vibrations of her tits and her bottom. The laziness of her steps did not seem to bother anybody. The audience treated her as if she was the star of all stars. Farida directed a suggestive glance towards the balcony, from which somebody threw down a red flower. She winked playfully back. This was when I noticed that the balconies were occupied by a few privileged men. They would have paid five pounds instead of two, and for this they had the luxury of having their drinks poured into the glasses that they would then raise in celebration of tired Farida, and the privilege of having their hubble-bubbles fed with burning coal by a younger version of our barman. Looking up at the privileged customers on their balcony, one could see that this theatre had enjoyed more prestigious times. The frontage of the balcony still bore traces of Gaudiesque decorations, and the ceiling must have impressed many a visitor in years gone by. The decline of this little showbiz heaven seemed to be obvious only to us, the two gender-different members of the audience. Everyone else had their eyes fixed on the performers and the charms they were so generously displaying for their benefit. By now Farida was busy shaking her tits and quivering her round parts for the sake of the man with the tiny body and the big, colourful hubble-bubble, who was smiling from behind his thick moustache. Farida was not young, but her admirers did not care, or maybe they did not notice. When people want to dream, nothing can stop them. When Farida left, dragging her feet and her heavy body slowly off the stage, a small, trim man dressed in vaudeville style, his face undecided between a Groucho Marx expression and a Clarke Gable finish, stepped to the middle of the stage to inform us that 'The Flower of Palestine is safely asleep at home, having sweet dreams.' This was presumably in case we were worried for the moral health of our young generation. 'The Flower of Palestine' was not to be allowed to watch Farida working at the titillation of her admirers.

Now the small man announced 'the purest voice of all, the sweetest of all singers, the Star of all Stars, the Nightingale of

East and West alike: Lubna, who will enchant you with a selection of songs.' Lubna arrived to the accompaniment of drum beats and loud whistles from the public. We two women were also applauding, and trying hopelessly to whistle, to the great surprise of our minders, who no longer knew what to make of us. Lubna's skin was fair and the dress she wore was so tight that her ample body seemed to come pouring out of it. Lubna was blond, too blond even for a Swedish woman. As she undulated her way generously to the centre of the stage, she announced the title of her first song: 'This is where I draw a red line.' The title of the song was clear, as was the meaning of her lines. Giving us a wonderfully suggestive smile, Lubna pointed at her lips and sang 'Here your kisses are welcome.' Then she repeated the words, still smiling, and pointed at her neck. Then at her enormous breasts. And finally, changing the expression on her face to a look of horror, she screamed rather than sang and crossed her hands on her tight dress at the level of her vagina. 'Here, never, your kisses will never be allowed. This is where I draw a red line.' The audience was completely mesmerized by her and when she indicated the forbidden zone, all the audience – all, that is, except us two women – cried in unison, 'Why not . . .? Why not . . .? Please Lubna.' Some said it pleadingly in all seriousness, others for the sake of the show, but most of them were half playing and half serious. Lubna had these males at her feet now, so she announced the title of her next song: 'I have no man, I need a man'.

I don't remember any of the tunes sung by 'The Star of all Stars'. I guess they didn't vary much from one song to the next. What changed was the audience's growing expectation for more obvious suggestiveness on the part of Lubna. Having expounded her longings for a man in two or three songs, she felt moved to continue her act flat on her back with her legs apart, singing as if in despair: 'I need a man, I need a man'. Her song became a summons. A call issuing from the desperation and fullness of her body. All the spectators stood up so as to see more of her: the privileged customers in the balcony leaned perilously over the rail. We women did not want to miss anything, so we stood up too, stretching upwards in order to have a better view of Lubna's act. Our minders had apparently forgotten us entirely, and they rushed to the front to stop some zealots who were trying to jump over onto the stage, screaming '*Ana, Ana*, Me! Me! I am here for you.' They did not have much trouble sending people back to their seats, for the fans were also, somehow, playing Lubna's game.

The French actress looked at her colleague, and then at me, and said, '*C'est du Molière, c'est du pur Molière.*' Her colleague, finally calming down along with the rest of the audience, sat back in his seat and declared: '*C'est ce qu'on appelle du happening. C'est ça le théâtre.*'

Lubna and Farida were the two high points of the evening. The show continued late into the night. We drank many Fantas that evening, and when the theatre closed its doors the city was still awake outside and warmly welcoming.

A few months later I read in a small item in the corner of the last page of an Arabic daily that a fire had broken out at Masrah Farouk and had destroyed the whole building. Nobody was hurt but the theatre had been closed until further notice. That was the end of Masrah Farouk, and soon after it died the war started.

Honour and Shame

Beirut has changed. You wouldn't recognize it if you came back. One thing is still the same as in the old days, though – those days when people like you were not afraid to stay and live in its chaotic beauty. The city still has a very lively transport network. Thousands of private cars, capable of taking up to five passengers apiece, circulate on routes whose logic is not immediately apparent. The cars stop to pick you up in the same way that a taxi would, and they drop you off wherever you want, even if this means holding up a queue of rush-hour traffic in the process. You pay the driver, at any time on the way, a fee which is agreed via a consensus arrived at by equally non-apparent processes. The important thing here is not the ingenuity of the system, or its anarchy, but the microcosm of life inside these cars over the distance of a few kilometres.

People of different class, sex and geographical origin are obliged to share a narrow space, their bodies squeezed one against the other: two next to the driver, and three on the back seat. This can be misery for a woman if she has the misfortune to end up sitting next to a groping male. He skilfully contrives to extend his allotted space so as to place a roving hand on the thigh of his female neighbour or to rub his thigh against hers.

What happens then depends on the character of the lady in question. She may shyly try to squeeze herself away next to the door, or closer to the other passenger, or she may come straight out and tell the man to go to hell for his lack of decency. If she opts for the latter approach, all the passengers in the car, the driver included, will feel it their duty to become involved, and they will start insulting the molester. Having been in such situations, I can tell you that the really skilled groper can make it very hard for you. The skilled molesters can be so subtle that when you glare at them, or try squeezing yourself away from them, they act as if they're just overly well-built, or hadn't realized that they were occupying more space than they should. Their eyes say that it was just an accident, and you should give people the benefit of the doubt. And if it's a borderline case, making a scene about decency – and having the other passengers insult the man for his lack of honour, with phrases like 'Have you no sister . . .? Have you no wife? Aren't you ashamed of insulting a woman's honour?' – may be a trifle unfair. My worst experience was when, armed with a feminist self-confidence freshly acquired from having read *The Female Eunuch*, I glared at the owner of an intruding hand that had landed subtly between my thighs, looked him in the eye and inquired as acidly as I could manage: 'Couldn't you find somewhere else to put your hand, instead of between my legs?' 'Oh sure,' he said with a dirty smile, 'but it's much nicer in there.'

Travelling for a few kilometres in one of these cars one learns a great deal about one's own society. If we had observed more closely as we rode in the common taxis – *Service*, as we call them – then we might have been more aware of the impending advent of the civil war. We might have thought more carefully about the aggression that erupted quite habitually in fights between two drivers whose 'rights' had come into conflict. Immediately before the war, a lot of car accidents ended up in bloodshed, because the outcome would be resolved and blame allocated by the guns that were pulled from the drivers' belts.

Earlier, when our society had been more stable, we had many times watched as a sweating *Service* driver got out of his car and physically threatened his opponent with the gesticulations of a man saying: 'Hold me back or God knows what I'll do to him.' There would always be enough volunteers among the passers-by to hold him and send him back to his car with a hearty slap on the back. Men had an ever-present need to show that they wouldn't let their pride be smashed without raising hell. It was no easy matter for a man to assert his manliness and honour in this city, where he had to drive for endless hours in the burning heat or through the flooded streets to make a living, to pay for all those attractive consumer goods, in the knowledge that security for his family's health and a decent education for his children were simply unattainable at any affordable price.

Honour, revenge and identity are all very intertwined in my country of origin. They took different forms, and even looked remote to many of us, with the modernisation and rapid cosmopolitanism of Lebanon, but they were there none the less. A mere ten or twenty miles from the capital Beirut, we still occasionally heard of a woman having been murdered because her brother or her father had decided to avenge their defiled honour with her blood. The power of blood and its ties and symbolism has not died in any human society. On the shores of the Mediterranean, blood still kills women, but elsewhere its sexual contamination still has the power to frighten even the most 'advanced' of societies into a state of hysteria. (When you request a entry visa to the USA, you are required to provide information about your HIV status.)

'Honour is in the eye of the beholder.' This was the prevalent attitude during my adolescence, in the place where I grew up. 'What would the neighbours say about us?' was a refrain that I heard almost every day. The NEIGHBOURS! If I acted in any way that failed to correspond to the norm (for instance if I was seen with some young man, or coming out of a cinema on my own, or being driven home late at night by friends who were not all female.) I would be giving reasons for others to question my honour. In a curious way, it didn't matter what I actually did. What mattered was who saw what, and how it might have been interpreted and, most important of all, how it was going to be reported. For the interpretation arrived at by neighbours and others would not concern me alone – it would affect all of my family, and they would be judged and blamed as readily as if they themselves had been seen doing the unthinkable. People would have reasons to speak badly of all of us.

In Arab Islamic societies it is very rare for people not to marry. Celibacy is considered to be anti-social, even anti-religious. So if a woman is single and seems to be in danger of staying unmarried, everybody around gets active in trying to marry her off. And they usually succeed. How many elder sisters have been given in marriage with threats such as: 'You have to behave. Your reputation has to be spotless. If you tarnish our image, your younger sisters will be left unmarried, and their spoiled lives will be a consequence of your actions.' Generally this kind of advice is forced onto a woman who rejects a suitor because he doesn't suit her, or who is on the verge of rebelling against a tyrannical husband.

If a distant relative died, whom I had possibly seen for no more than ten minutes in my whole life, I was expected to dress in black for at least forty days. Otherwise, people – the neighbours, the shopkeepers, the hairdresser at the street corner – would blame my whole family for my scandalous behaviour. This obsessive fear of the threatening word *sharaf* (honour) was there both in the family's frightened eyes and in the neighbours' curious scrutiny.

This word and its inflated power also appeared in school, in the French Lycée. But here it came with the smirk on the lips of the teacher. Monsieur Pierre, the enthusiastic young socialist French *cooperant* with whom most of us girls were slightly in love, fed us values that were imbued with the French republican spirit: 'Montesquieu said that Honour is a typically monarchical value. Republican government is based on virtue and respect for the law.' Worse than that, M. Pierre, who charmed us all – and whom I am sure you would have appreciated, had you not left the country – had a favourite saying by Racine, which he often quoted in the classroom: 'Without money, honour is nothing but a sickness.' In school we all had to learn by heart the tragic lines of Don Diegue in *Le Cid*: *O rage, O désespoir, O vieillesse ennemie – N'ai-je donc vécu que pour cette infamie* ... The whole poem had something of a folkloric taste in our recently modernized minds. When we recited it we thought of M. Pierre, and we accompanied the verses with over-exaggerated gestures, turning tragedy into comedy. The word *infamies* in particular often had us falling over our desks with laughter.

However, in our Lycée Français the word 'honour' was far from remote. It featured in all its glory on the *Tableau d'Honneur*, which was (and still is) a sort of ritual which rewards the individual's work and cleverness in the same way that criminals are branded, by exhibiting their names publicly for all to see. Honour, in the view of our French school, was something acquired through effort, work and excellence, not through the sword or virginal chastity, or matters of blood. Our teachers had been 'contaminated' by the now unavoidable influence of psychology and relativism in the judgement of human behaviour. Now Bad and Good needed longer and less assertive phrases in order to be defined. They were, we were once told by M. Pierre, often interchangeable, according to the position from which you looked at them.

At school nobody ever suggested that the opinions of one's neighbours might be a value reference. For some of us the dichotomy between what we were taught in the French lycée and the reality of our home surroundings was somehow schizophrenic; for others it was a good source of maturity and investigative thinking. Mind you, a mild form of schizophrenia operated in the school itself. Certain of the teachers still set up systems whereby one of the students would inform on others (this was so that the teachers could leave the class in silence for a while if they had to take care of other business). The teacher appointed one of the students to be responsible for discipline.

The student would go to the blackboard and write down the names of fellow students who were talking or misbehaving. Others of the teachers would have despised any student who told on others and often spoke of solidarity as a prime matter of honour. It is easy, at first sight, to condemn a student who causes the punishment of his fellow classmates. Most decent, enlightened parents would tend that way. But ask these same liberal-minded parents if they would want their children to tell on a fellow schoolmate who was walking around promoting drugs and you will find that in the rare cases when the answer is not positive, it will be hesitant and much less readily forthcoming.

Tell a half smart, modern-educated city person that they are virtuous and honourable and they will think that you see them as some kind of fake, or a poser, or a relic from the past. Obviously I am exaggerating but honour is suspect in this age of psychotherapy and coexistence. The comforting phrases: We may be poor, but at least can be proud of our reputation . . . We are poor but we are clean . . . We are poor but we never harmed anybody . . . We may be poor, but our name knows no blemish . . . are less and less convincing. The concern about establishing dignity and justice is an unclear and convoluted business in what we call our Big Village.

Is this the ambiguity that lies at the root of our fascination with the Mafia and its codes of honour? Why do we watch *The Godfather* films again and again? Not merely for the exoticism and colour of the frightening and exciting underworld that they portray. We watch them because it is easy to fall into the convincing, self-sealed and harmonious values of honour and revenge that these Men of Their Words have set for themselves. And we are constantly reminded that such rigidly demanding codes of honour cannot function without an accompanying and overwhelming set of betrayals. We know this about life, but here it is blown up into a larger dimension, and the blood flows more freely than usual.

The Revenge of Leila's Grandmother

Do you remember Leila, Mrs Nomy? She was the happy, talkative girl who shared my desk. The girl that I had chosen as my best friend with the enthusiasm that only little girls know. She understood better than I did your anger over my little story.

Leila's grandmother was not like other grandmothers. She was much thinner and more imposing than other grandmothers I had seen. She never treated Leila's friends to nice cakes, folk stories or generous, loving smiles. The older we grew the thinner she became, and the longer her neck seemed. She held her neck as you hold a stick in front of you, always tilted slightly forward. She rarely said a nice word to any of us, and when she did, we were never sure, Leila and I, that she really meant to be pleasant. Her name was Fadwa. She was an erect, nervous presence who filled me with confusion and unease, for I had not been told that this was how some grandmothers could be.

I will never forget Leila's grandma. She created confusion into my youthful naivety, and it was only when I met Leila again, in London, in my late thirties, that I understood this perennially bony, taut and elongated woman. She was a woman who fed on anger, and she drew her energies from an insatiable need for revenge. Her husband had betrayed her in the early years of their marriage, and she could never forgive him the humiliation. After her grandmother's death, Leila told me the story of this woman whom we had so hated and feared. She spoke about her with a newly felt compassion and even some humour.

Fadwa was born at the turn of the century. Nobody really knew the exact date. When identity cards were introduced in Lebanon she was already a teenager, a fact that made her insist, throughout her life that the registration office had made her a few years older than she really was. She often told Leila how beautiful she had been in her youth. Then she would pause and wait for her granddaughter's inevitable response: 'But you are still a beautiful woman, Grandma.' Up there in the mountains, above the Bekaa Valley, the First World War was experienced mainly through the hunger and the misery that it brought to the peasants. 'But we never lacked anything in our family,' Fadwa insisted. 'While everyone around us was starving, we had plenty of grain in our attic, whole jars of olive oil, and soaps and perfumed incense. We were a cut above the average villager.'

So Fadwa believed, or liked to believe, for in 1916, when she was still an adolescent, her parents shipped her off on a boat to Ghana, where she was to meet her new husband, Salem, an earlier immigrant who had a business there and whom she had not met previously. It was a fate no different from that of many other girls of her time. In order to save them from hunger, the parents located a family with an immigrant son, with whom they arranged their daughter's marriage. In fact Fadwa thought she was going to America, for that was what people called Africa in her village. The reason for this geographical confusion was simple. People in the villages would pay a boat owner a certain sum of money to take their children to America, which was supposed to be the land of wealth and opportunities. The ship owner would disembark his ignorant passengers on any shore that happened to suit him, telling them: 'Here you are. This is America.'

This was how Fadwa's future husband had ended up in Ghana. There he had opened a shop, in which he sold bananas as well as costume jewellery, medicines, tinned sardines and cosmetic creams that promised an eternally youthful complexion. He needed a wife who would give him a home and a family and, most importantly, recreate for him a bit of the Lebanese village that he had left behind and for which he still deeply longed.

Before sending her off alone on the boat, Fadwa's mother had told her over and over again that she should watch out for men *en route*. There were too many stories of lives that had been destroyed because of young girls making silly mistakes during these lonely journeys. The honour of the family, who had given their word to Salem's family, was at stake. 'You are the most beautiful girl among these hungry peasants,' her mother told her repeatedly before her departure. 'We fed you well. You are going to marry this Salem. Be a good wife to him, but never forget that our family is far superior to his. Before he opened his shop in America his parents never even had one full jar of oil in their attic. Let him know, and let everybody know, that he is about to marry a girl from a home that his family could never even have dreamt of visiting before the war.'

In those days Fadwa was already slim and tall for her age. But her edge was not yet as hard, and her neck was still more elegant than tense. She landed with a large brown cloth bag into which she had packed three dresses, some underwear, a bottle of olive oil and four bags of grain, before tying its four corners in a safe knot which she would use as a handle. The pink dress she was wearing looked fancy to the other peasants, but didn't impress the crew of the boat, who had seen more recent fashions during their stopovers at the world's ports.

Fadwa was full of apprehension before her first meeting with Salem, but her mother's words had had their effect. She would show him that she had come down in the world in marrying him. Salem tried to be nice, but he had little time for Fadwa's dreams and not much experience with young women's expectations either. They married in Africa, which they still called America in their letters to their families back in the village. At first they seemed to get along well. Salem wished that Fadwa would gain some weight. She, for her part, wished that he would dress in different clothes when he left the shop, and act like someone who had married into a better family than the others in the Lebanese community around them. She began to grow a round belly, which had a curiously distended look as it stretched out from her bony body. Salem often went to the club to play cards after work, while Fadwa went through the pains of nausea and back aches. She went on for many years like that, bearing children and taking care of the little ones. Her opinion was that he ought to worship her for having provided him with this big male family: one girl and five healthy boys, along with only two miscarriages in twelve years. She was convinced that now, since she was the mother of his five boys, and since she was from a far better family than him, Salem would be more than grateful to her. But Fadwa's repeated pregnancies had had a drastic effect on her body. She was now just an angular shadow of a woman. Instead of making her hips rounder and giving her belly the smooth, fuller contours that most women acquire after childbirth, Fadwa's body was extending upwards, nervously and tightly, making her look taller and less approachable than ever.

Dr Day, the British doctor who had opened a clinic in the town almost a year before her last pregnancy, insisted that she should not consider another birth. Fadwa had lived a life of isolation, bounded by new-born babies and repeated pregnancies, for as long as she could remember. Salem was grateful, but did not change his manners. Nor did he get round to wearing shoes on Sundays, as she kept asking. Instead he wore sandals which exposed his big tilted toes.

Fadwa refused to mix with the other Lebanese families in their immigrant community. She didn't want her children to acquire what she considered to be unsuitable manners. She would have liked to have invited Dr Day and his family round, but he never had time to chat, and his wife never came to the clinic, so Fadwa couldn't invite the doctor's children to play with her own. She hadn't been seeing much of Salem lately. He tended to stay at the club. The more his shop prospered the more help he hired, both for the shop and the house, and the less she saw of him. 'I had more than ten boys serving me there,' she would say resentfully, after she returned home hurriedly during the first wave of African nationalism. They left together with many other prosperous merchant families. Back in her village Fadwa would look disdainfully at her only maid. She ordered her around as if it was her fault that she had no cook or serving boys, whatever they'd been called, not like what she'd had in what was, by then, finally known as Africa.

On the day of their departure, while the slogans and chants of the mass demonstrations could be heard from the dining room, Salem came to tell Fadwa that they all had to leave. They could leave unharmed as long as they left everything behind to make it look as if they were going for a short visit downtown. He would follow the family very shortly and meet them in London. The hotel was already booked. Fadwa didn't even have time to ask questions. She found herself in the back of a truck, with her children, and the thick wad of money that Salem had told her to hide between her breasts. This was only the beginning of her misery. The truth that she was about to discover a few hours later would hit her in the face like a sharp, humiliating blow. From that moment on, her need for revenge would never be satisfied; it would be the motive behind every movement she made, the source of every thought she could think and the taste of every bit of air she breathed.

There she was, in the queue at the airport, with all the other Lebanese families, waiting for the first available plane to take them out of the country. She had Walid, her two-year-old, on one arm, and a big plastic bag on the other. As she looked around for her other five children, for fear of losing them in the chaos of the queue, she heard words that fell on her heart like a burning stone. It was the wife of Khalid speaking. 'Salem is not with Fadwa.' 'Obviously not,' said Amina, whom Fadwa had never liked, and who dared think of herself as higher class than Fadwa herself. 'He would never leave that woman of his and her daughter behind. He would leave his whole family, to stay with his lover and their daughter. He has no shame about it. Poor Fadwa.' POOR FADWA. Those words whirled round the airport and whirled in her ears like a fly caught inside a lampshade. She'd never had a clue, she'd never had the slightest suspicion. Everyone else seemed to know all about it. They must all have gossiped about it with the same disgusting smile that she saw at the corner of Amina's lips.

She had no idea how she had landed in London, or how she had arrived at the hotel. The noises of the aircraft and the noises of her demanding children were all mixed in with the buzzing of the words that were spinning in her ears and in her head, and weighing on her chest. Everyone knew about it, everyone except her. These women, whom she would never have condescended to mix with, were holding conversations about her misery. She would rather have died than live to face such an affront.

He, Salem, was the one responsible for her affront. Him, that sandal-wearing peasant, who should have kissed her feet for all that she had done for him. She thought of the children with whom he had left her alone, in this damp, miserable city, and this intimidating hotel. She would not wait for him in

London; she would go back to the village and once she got there she would let him know who he really was and who was worth what.

Salem did in fact come back. A month late, and a few years older. He looked like a broken man. A man who had lost everything he cherished and everything he had worked for. A month is a long time in anybody's life, and it was more than enough for somebody as hurt as Fadwa to turn their village home into *her* home. Enough to turn the children into *her* children, and the main bedroom into a two-bedded room where Salem would feel like an intruder forever after. From the moment he arrived back in the village with his suitcase full of dirty, wrinkled shirts, he became HE for Fadwa. From then on, right up until his death, she would never again pronounce his name, never address him directly. 'HE is too tired to come out visiting with us,' she would say. 'He cannot eat sweet things, they're bad for him,' she would declare, as she spirited away the baklava that she knew he adored. If some cousin of his ever came to visit, she would make sure that they never came back a second time. She made sure that whenever anyone came to see Salem they realised that they were unwanted, and that they were looked down upon because of their lower social status. Fadwa was never impolite or rude. On the contrary, she always acted like a modest wife and a perfect mother. But people who came to see Salem never came back again. Salem, on the other hand, was never allowed to go out on his own. Either Fadwa would be with him or, if he ever made an independent foray, she would make him pay dearly for it. Anyway, since his return to the village his health seemed to have abandoned him. By now he was more African than Lebanese, and he had not realised that what he was suffering from was his inability to integrate into a country that he had only ever known as a child.

Salem may have felt estranged in the new setting of his Lebanese home, but Fadwa did not really relax or blossom either. True, she seemed in control, but the effort of it all was tensing her face and making it more severe, her movements were becoming even more angular and her voice was becoming sour and angular too. The children were her children now, and she made sure that she possessed every single movement they made, every single desire they had. What she was really good at was standing between them and their father, making sure that direct contact was either impossible or a source of guilt for them. None of them was ever to marry anyone they desired, or even could have liked. Whenever she felt that one of the boys was drawn to a young, attractive woman, she would become restless and find ways to bring ugliness into the situation. Only her daughter ended up marrying the person of her choice. This further embittered Fadwa, but she could live with it, since she knew, as everybody knew, that it is not through daughters that women gain power in this part of the world. The wives of the five sons were chosen for their lack of charm and attractiveness. They were to be pitied for their weakness and lack of influence, and this was precisely what Fadwa wanted.

Fadwa developed an obsession with cleanliness. She was forever telling the maid to go and wash her hands. She could be seen most of the time scrubbing and dusting and cleaning germs off things. It was hard to tell whether her bony, emaciated hands were hardened from all that scrubbing, or whether those sad hands were doing the only thing that her angry eyes could direct them to do – cleaning the dirt that only she could see, and that she believed she had to destroy before it destroyed her. Fadwa would scrub, and as she scrubbed she would look at Salem with loathing. She saw harm in everything he enjoyed. For instance when he sat on the balcony at dusk. 'He can't do that . . . he'll catch cold,' she would say, and one of the sons would have to bring his father back into the small sitting room where she kept him penned. If she felt he was enjoying a song on the radio, she would say: 'He should turn that off. I don't want that kind of degenerate music in my home.'

For a further twenty-five years Fadwa shared the same home and slept in the same room as Salem, without ever uttering his name or addressing a word to him, or letting up the onslaught that she had launched against him the day she'd heard those terrible words at the airport. The words swirled unceasingly in her head, with a force that fed her anger and kept her energies constantly renewed. She scrubbed to their rhythm and hated with their force. She moved restlessly all the time, as though she wouldn't be able to rub away her humiliation if she stayed still.

Fadwa would not let go. The more miserable Salem looked, the more broken he appeared, the stronger she felt, and the more determined grew her will to punish him. In the last two years before his death, when he was confined to a wheelchair and had lost all taste for life, she took away the only little pleasure he still had: the meals that broke the loneliness of his days, with their long hours of apathy and boredom. Fadwa decided that a good healthy menu was what 'the old man', as she had started to call him, needed, in order to live a bit longer. She knew what he most particularly loathed – vegetable and lamb stews. So she restricted his diet to this one item. Leila was once caught and severely punished for having treated him to a piece of chocolate. 'That's all he needs now, to start complaining of stomach aches and making my life even more of a misery,' Fadwa had screamed, beside herself with anger.

By now, Salem was actively looking forward to leaving this world, as a way of escaping Fadwa's ministrations. I visited Leila the week before he died, and I still remember the way that his eyes seemed to show a new purpose. They showed a spark of life, for they were the eyes of a man who had made a decision. He would take away from Fadwa her means of hurting him. He died suddenly in his wheelchair, with no prior signs or warning.

Fadwa was restless during the funeral. She had the look of precisely what she was – a person who would not let go. She was agitated, and seemed intent on prolonging the mourning rituals and directing the ceremonials. 'True, the man was a big burden, but he might have lived a bit longer,' she said. Her lips were taut. 'I always did my best to look after him.'

Fadwa did not outlive Salem by much. Her energies seemed to dwindle rapidly. Her bitterness had no focus, and without active revenge she had nothing else on which to feed. Revenge had become the whole substance of her life. As a result, the death of Salem left her with new feelings of betrayal. She had lived out of hatred, a hatred that she had nourished with his misery. Fadwa had never made space in her heart, or in her body, for any other source of life energy. When the end came, she died mumbling something about feeling a lump in her throat. It was the betrayal that she had never been able to swallow, and the revenge that she had never been able to exact.

The Heroism of Umm Ali

When Hayat told me that the famous Umm Ali was none other than Latifa, the little maid who used to live in their home, I found myself feeling confused and depressed. For me, Latifa would always be the frail, skinny little girl who used to have to stand on a stool in the big, damp kitchen in order to reach the sink where piles of dirty dishes and pans seemed to accumulate unendingly. Latifa had been nine years old when I started going to the dark stuffy flat where Hayat lived with her father, his mother, his second wife and her son. I used to go round after school to do my homework. Like all the little girls who worked as maids in Beirut, Latifa woke up before everybody else, and only went to sleep after the last of them had gone to bed. She was both the youngest and the smallest in the establishment, and she was there to clean, scrub and bear the brunt of the family's anger, their whims and their insults. Hayat was the only one who ever expressed any measure of sympathy towards this little girl, this taken-for-granted slave in this miserable three-bedroom flat. Latifa slept in the kitchen and here she had to carry her mattress every night before settling down into the deep sleep of little girls of her age. Hayat's sympathy, however, did little to better Latifa's lot, because it was stored passively – in her eyes and her downcast look, the only refuge that Hayat had for her feelings.

The image of Umm Ali, the new-born legend on the fighting streets of Beirut, the ruthless fighter who knew neither fear nor compassion, 'the sister of men' as they named her, was already well sketched in my mind, and I could find no way of relating this ferocious, aggressive character to the frightened, evasive little nine-year-old Latifa that I had known. Umm Ali was large and powerful in my imagination, whereas in my memory Latifa was still victimised and vulnerable. The atrocious absurdity of a civil war settling indefinitely all around you may confuse your sense of reality, and it can definitely upset your moral judgements, but there is one thing that it cannot permeate – the memories that preceded it, which are etched into the person that you are now. The amputated childhood of Latifa, the child, had been my first encounter with heartlessness and abject despotism. My own childhood was not far behind me when I began visiting Hayat's gloomy home, and Latifa had settled into my otherwise carefree and happy adolescence like a sad and long-borne wound which never permitted me to enjoy my relative privilege.

Latifa was brought to Beirut by her father and her elder brother, from a village in the north, up by the Syrian border. They had come to place her in 'a respectable home, with good people,' as they put it. As if she was a business proposition. People who would pay an advance on her as a sign of goodwill, and then pay them a monthly fee for her services as a maid from then onwards. They pronounced that they had heard good things about Mr Farid and his lady, Umm Wisam – Hayat's father, in other words, and his second wife – about their good reputation and their generosity. They were in no doubt that Latifa would be well fed, treated fairly, and given new clothes on the feast days, as well as being taught respect for traditional and family values and fear of God's wrath for wrongdoing. They concurred that Latifa was too young to be granted a day off on Sundays.'Where would she go on her own? The town is too dangerous for a girl her age. After all, she's never been away from her mother's skirt until today.' Umm Wisam, a shrewd bargainer, put on a sceptical air. 'She's too thin. We'll need to feed her up before she can even start working.' She was already thinking of the advance and the girl's monthly wage. The argument over the fees went on for a long time, and foundered every time Latifa's father refused to consider what he called a humiliating proposal or when Umm Wisam declared that she wasn't really that interested after all. The brother and Farid then expatiated respectively on the subject of Farid's honourable family – 'which matters to us more than the money' – or about how 'Latifa would never find a woman as compassionate and undemanding as my wife.' Finally the deal was sealed, the money changed hands, and Latifa was now living in a new world, among people she knew nothing about, away from her mother's arms, and a thousand years away from her childhood.

At the end of the following month, her father showed up on a Sunday afternoon as agreed. He was drunk. He took Latifa's first wages, leaving her in no doubt that it was *his* money. He didn't bother to take Latifa out, nor did he ask how she was doing or feeling. Umm Wisam couldn't bear his breath, which was heavy with cheap alcohol, and his loud voice, which was 'that of an unemployed peasant'. She convinced Farid and a very willing father that there was no need for them to come for their money. Instead it would be delivered to the village via the taxi driver, the self-appointed middle-man who had originally brokered the deal. Latifa was left there, abandoned by a father who had never wanted her, taken away from a mother who had never had any say and who was not able to defend her, and given to a family who could hardly make ends meet and who had no space in their flat – let alone in their hearts – for anyone as destitute and vulnerable as this nine-year-old girl.

When Latifa was brought into Farid's home, Umm Wisam was going through a very unhappy transformation in her life and status. She had always resented the permanent presence of her mother-in-law in her flat. She felt that it created a confusion as to who was the first lady in the house. Her mother-in-law occupied the largest room in the flat. She intervened in every little detail of the running of the household, and of Farid's life and his relationship with his wife. And worst of all, she seemed to take it for granted that no social gathering initiated by Umm Wisam could happen without her being right there in the middle. And now, just when she had finally won her battle against Farid's first wife, making sure that Farid visited her only rarely, and ignoring her complaints and advice, she discovered that Farid was thinking of entering into a third marriage. After fifteen years of their marriage, Farid was apparently wanting to exercise his right to acquire another wife.

The more Umm Wisam lost ground, the more demanding and venomous she became. She resented everyone who lived in the flat. All except her fourteen-year-old only son Wisam.

Him she spoiled, showering him with attention and adoration. He was her winning weapon in her fight against her first rival, who had given Farid only female offspring – three daughters. He was the only man in her life whom she could claim as entirely her own. Wisam was growing fast, in both girth and length. He became used to being treated like a little Pasha, and also to failing at school. Latifa became his scapegoat, and the focus of his and his mother's frustrations.

Wisam and his mother felt exploited if Latifa was not seen working in the flat, which only happened very rarely.

'We are not paying your father vast sums of money just for you to be fed and pampered.' Such remarks Umm Wisam would throw at Latifa each time she saw her looking through the window at the children playing in the courtyard.

Then, in the evening, after she had cleared the dining table, washed the dishes and cleaned the kitchen, Latifa would sit discreetly near the door of the living room to watch, with the rest of the family, one of the Egyptian sagas that occupied the TV screens and the imagination of the whole neighbourhood. But after a while the boy Wisam would order her to fetch him a bottle of Coca Cola from the shop downstairs, or his mother would tell her to go and make sure everything was neat and tidy. Latifa would obey and bury her sadness silently inside her big eyes.

Latifa was alone in her misery, and she was to be alone in her tragedy. Wisam was big and arrogant. He was becoming a man. The worst was bound to happen. One morning Latifa failed to move her mattress from the kitchen. Despite the calls of the grandmother demanding her morning tea – which Latifa always brought to her bedroom, where the smell of her wet tobacco mixed with that of her stale biscuits – and despite the threat of Umm Wisam's retribution, Latifa stayed in bed, hiding under the faded pink quilt. Wisam had come into the kitchen during the night. There was blood on the mattress, confusion in Latifa's head, and terror in her body. Farid and his wife became hysterical. Farid went looking for Wisam, who was not in the flat. Umm Wisam started accusing Latifa of having bewitched her son, of having tried to destroy the life of her wonderful child. Hayat left the flat and went to stay with her mother, who had no room for her in her flat. Voices were hushed in the three-bedroom flat, and the shutters were kept closed for fear of alarming the neighbours.

Hayat told me later that Wisam had been punished – his father had reduced his pocket money by half, despite the mother's objections. And Farid had started spending more time at his third wife's flat. Nobody thought of consoling Latifa, whose eyes grew bigger and whose movements became more tense. She was forbidden to leave the flat, and was not sent out on errands for a long time after what they referred to as 'the accident'. She was taken to a secret clinic to be 'restored', and regained her virginity through a stitching operation. Wisam was given money to go downtown, where prostitutes would solve his problems and bear the burden of his heavy body and his bad manners. Latifa was given a wage rise in expectation of a parental visit, which usually took place when her father had accumulated drinking debts. And there Latifa stayed, in that flat that was turning darker than ever, for Umm Wisam kept cluttering it with fresh objects to fill the space that was left by Farid's increasing absences.

I stopped going to Hayat's flat. It was like hell. I could no longer stand the smell of stale biscuits, and the glittering arrays of knick-knacks that Latifa had to dust every day. But most of all I could no longer tolerate Hayat's submissive tolerance of her family's meanness. I should have looked deeper into Latifa's eyes, instead of just bringing her secret supplies of sweets. Maybe, through their anxious stare, I would have seen the immense power that was swelling up, fed by her desire to escape from this hostile hole into which she had been thrown. It was not because of her anguish that her eyes were looking larger; they were feverishly, secretly searching for a way out. To a place where warm voices would whisper sweetly in her ears: Here you belong, here we want you to be among us, here you are one of us.

The civil war that sprang upon the country very soon engulfed the neighbourhood in which Farid's second home was located. The stagnant, cosy routines of its inhabitants were so abruptly disrupted, and their streets turned so easily into an apocalyptic battlefield, that it was as if it had all happened under the spell of some magician's wand. The settled little hierarchies of these petty bourgeois clerks, these shopkeepers and their families, were suddenly huddled into anguished corridors and damp cellars, in which their status was squeezed as well as their bodies. The powerful and the less powerful, the compassionate and the unfeeling, the arrogant and the timid were brought to one same, common level in their struggle for survival. Nothing of what had once been mattered any longer, in the apocalyptic fires that governed their fate at this moment. They all feared the streets, and submitted willingly to the chaos of control by trigger-happy fighters. Umm Wisam knew that if her son were to join one of the militias that had settled in the neighbourhood she would have less reason to fear for her home and possessions – but she was too attached to him, and more than anything she feared the loss of her control over him once he got his hands on a rifle and began mixing with those men who never seemed to have homes to go to.

It was inevitably Latifa who got sent to fetch bread from the bakery when it was too dangerous to face the shelling and when snipers had emptied the busy streets of shoppers. When Farid's family rushed down to the basement, alarmed by the closeness of battle and the wheezing criss-cross of the gunfire, it was she who was sent back to the flat to fetch the blankets, or the grandmother's prayer *masbaha*, or Farid's medicine, or sometimes even the box of stale biscuits. As it happened, Latifa did not mind. On the contrary, she took her time as she went upstairs, savouring the silent emptiness of the flat. She even enjoyed being sent to the bakery, because from there she could watch the movement of the fighters as they crossed the street in zigzag formation to join their comrades in the basement next to the bakery which they had chosen as their headquarters. She felt no fear, but breathed an air of freedom in the new shape that the streets had acquired. She would soon be seventeen, which meant that she had been confined for almost eight years in this same street, with the narrow, unchanging view from the kitchen on the second floor where she lived. She found the changes that were now transforming this familiar, monotonous sight welcome and exhilarating. The threatening flash and thunder of the falling shells did not affect her; they were just a secondary backdrop to her newly acquired spaces.

Every morning she stayed a bit longer at the baker's shop. She began to chat with the militiamen as they relaxed at the door of their headquarters. They had a special self-confidence in their expressions when informing the bakery customers about the military situation in the area, and of their plans for the neighbourhood's defence. Their bold, authoritative attitude with anyone arriving at the bakery fascinated Latifa. They spoke to her in the same familiar tone in which they spoke with Sitt Saniya, Umm Wisam's friend. Sitt Saniya had no maid, but was forever complaining about 'them' during her frequent visits to Umm Wisam before the war. Sitt Saniya was a familiar face at the *sobhiya*, the morning visit, along with two or three other housewives who lived in the same building or nearby. They would crowd into the living room, which looked even narrower with the *nargileh* and their babies, and would begin by exchanging compliments with Umm Wisam. The conversation would then develop into lengthy complaints about the shameful behaviour and lack of decency of all the people they knew and had never liked. Umm Wisam would tell them with rancour about Farid's new wife, who was far worse than his first wife, and who was draining him of every penny he had, because she was from a very low background . . . and . . . and . . . . But always, without exception, these gatherings would end up in unanimous castigation of the laziness of maids who 'think they deserve to be treated like little princesses' and who 'are starting to make demands, as if we're the maids and they're the mistresses'. When Latifa entered the living room with freshly heated charcoal to fuel the *nargileh*, or to serve Turkish coffee, the conversation would hardly be interrupted, for all the ladies in the gathering knew who 'they' was meant to refer to. So did Latifa, and that is why she loved the way the fighters spoke to Mrs Saniya: casually, and with no special respect. Latifa needed passionately to be like them, to become one of them.

One morning, upon being informed that the militia downstairs intended to mobilise all the young men in the neighbourhood, Umm Wisam went hysterical. She began hurling insults about gangsters and good-for-nothing thugs hanging about with their guns, and she asked Farid for money to be able to send her son away and protect him from such threats to his life. Wisam was now in his early twenties, and was neither in education nor out of it. His father was trying to find him a job as a clerk in the ministry where he himself was a clerk. But nothing was functioning normally in the country. It was a period of abnormality, in which men spent more time in their homes than in their offices, and students rarely attended courses. So Wisam was forever hanging about the house. Umm Wisam thought of enlisting the sympathy of the fighters who were threatening to enrol her son and take him away from her. She started preparing meals and the occasional large tray of soggy sweets as a treat for them. She would tell Latifa: 'Go and take this food to the fighters downstairs. Tell them that Umm Wisam wishes them good luck, and thanks them for protecting us, and prays for God to support them in their courageous battle.' Latifa was overwhelmed with excitement at the prospect of going inside the fighters' 'home' – which was what she called their headquarters. She carried the trays with great care and immense enthusiasm. She carried the food down as if it were a treasure she had just discovered and was exhibiting to the world. Her heart was pounding and her steps were light and long. She sensed that her fate was about to change, and that her life in Umm Wisam's kitchen was already far behind her, in a past that she had no wish to remember.

The fighters' home was spacious and bare except for a few mattresses piled up in one corner and the Kalashnikovs lying next to the three men who were sitting on the floor. Latifa made a great effort to hide the emotions whirling inside her. The words spilled out in a torrent. 'This food is for you ... I am a fighter too ... I want to stay with you.' She had rehearsed these words so many times that she wasn't aware of how strange she must have looked, and how abrupt she must have sounded to the three men as they sat there relaxing between 'missions'. She explained how eager she was to be one of them, to face the enemy, and how she did not fear the enemy and was eager to destroy him. She told them that she was willing to live in this 'home' and leave it only to accomplish 'missions', however dangerous or perilous they might be. When she realised that they were hesitating, she insisted that they follow her outside, where they could see for themselves what she meant. The street was empty near the bakery – none of the local people would even venture onto it, let alone cross it, for fear of falling victim to a sniper who had killed three people the day before and was still terrorising the district from his unknown location. Without warning Latifa dived into the street and ran in a zigzag as she had so often seen the fighters do as she watched from her kitchen window. She stopped on the other side and raised her hand to flash a V-sign at the source of the stream of bullets that had missed her. Then, without hesitation, she zigzagged back through a fresh hail of bullets. The three men started firing randomly in the direction of the sniper, and as they ducked behind the bakery door they applauded and whistled with admiration. Latifa had made her point and won her bet. From that moment on she was to be called Umm Ali, the sister of men. Latifa learned that if she wanted to fit in with these men she had to build her image as the girl who knew no fear – always the first to confront the enemy and the last to flee danger. She knew that the only way for her to belong was by turning herself into a legend.

I have no way of knowing how Umm Ali felt among all these men – how free she felt in their smoky presence, eating tinned food, drinking tea through the night, and sleeping at odd hours of the day on one of the sheetless mattresses. She wore their fighting clothes and carried one of their kalashnikovs on her shoulder. Her head was always covered with a *keffiya*, and her body flattened and anonymous under heavy military attire. People said that her voice had turned coarse and her manners rough. Like her comrades, she would shout brusquely at anyone who happened to get in their way, ordering them to clear the street for the passage of their showy, open-top jeeps. Some now claim that they recognised her big inquisitive eyes. 'Those eyes would betray her every effort at concealment.' Her eyes were those of the combatants who kept watch throughout that terrible night when nobody dared sleep. These were the fighters who kept their fingers on the trigger, sending endless streams of bullets in all directions while their bodies stood miraculously steady and their posture unshakable. Latifa's eyes were the only feature in her body that defied her efforts at total transformation, and resisted the creation of her new persona.

'I'd recognise her arrogant stare at a distance of a thousand kilometres,' said Mrs Saniya to Umm Wisam. 'You can go and claim her back. It's your right.' Umm Wisam would act as if she'd lost interest in the whole business, and with a dismissive gesture of her hand she would shrug off the idea of bringing Latifa back to the flat. 'God forgive her . . . Even if she comes begging me to take her back, I'll tell her sorry, no. My husband has daughters, and we all know what the presence of a girl like this can do to their reputation, when they've shamelessly spent their days and nights with all kinds of men . . .' Umm Wisam shrugged her shoulders too abruptly for a person who didn't really care. Actually she was terribly afraid of Latifa and of the secrets that she might be revealing to her new comrades. 'These people might listen to her lies and try to harm my son,' she would say to Farid whenever they were on their own. 'The snake tried to seduce my Wisam, and since she failed to trick him into marrying her, she might come and take her revenge. She might attack our home . . . steal our valuables . . . set fire to it. There's a lot of that kind of thing happening nowadays . . .'

Nobody could tell which of the stories told about Umm Ali were real and which were the fruit of people's imagination. The war was breeding a triumphant morbidity. It sealed absurd alliances and then turned them without warning into meaningless and bloody feuds. The rule of the arbitrary and the victory of chaos opened the way for people's imaginations to run riot, expanding along with their fears and their frantic attempts to exorcise them. Latifa, the young maid had crossed the sacred line that separates the sexes and defines their difference. Latifa the poor servant who moved as if constantly frightened by her own shadow was now walking and running through the streets as if she owned them. Her boldness, her disturbing audacity seemed to symbolize the new fate of the city. Nothing was secure or sacred any longer. People's lives, homes and destinies could be, and were being, suddenly turned upside down. Latifa no longer needed to do anything to preserve her reputation as a bold and fearless combatant. People who knew her, and those who only knew her by repute, were happy to inflate her legend. In their terrified lives only monsters and saints made sense, and only heroes and martyrs seemed cut out for survival.

Umm Ali became a favourite topic of conversation in the shelters and the narrow corridors where people took refuge. People spoke loudly in these shelters, as if trying to beat the terrible thunder of battle with their voices, and they all spoke at once to prove to themselves that they need fear no danger in loneliness.

Umm Ali was seen in many places at the same time. Once somebody had seen her in an Israeli jail, having allegedly been captured during a daring action inside 'enemy territory'. But in those same days there were also tales of her exploits in the battle of the hotels in downtown Beirut. These exploits invaded people's minds and dreams. Umm Ali was neither woman nor man. Latifa was no longer the vulnerable little maid. The perplexed confusion that her name evoked fitted well with the tumult and chaos that was everywhere. Life and death were now closely bound together, and it was as if they created another reality. Why should not Latifa the girl, now become Umm Ali the very manly woman, be present simultaneously in places that were widely distant?

Umm Ali died. Nobody knows how or under what circumstances. One morning the baker asked Umm Wisam if she had any pictures of 'the martyr Umm Ali', when she was still Latifa. Umm Wisam was mightily relieved to hear of her death, because she was still convinced that Umm Ali would be coming to harm her and her son. Latifa had never had her picture taken. She died as faceless as she had lived, with features that were of no concern to the dead among whom she now numbered. Umm Ali was a legend too, and she had no features either. The walls of Beirut would not miss another picture; they were already too busy and had no space for latecomers. A martyr needs a face and a name, and Latifa had no family name. What her detractors never understood was that she had no wish for revenge. She looked beyond life, instead of looking back into it. She stepped into another reality and had no desire to remember the ugliness that had suffocated her. Umm Ali could have easily returned the humiliations that Latifa had suffered in Farid's home. She could easily have spilled blood enough to cover all the mattresses in that wretched flat where she had once been made to bleed. But all she had wanted was to forget the smell of stale biscuits, the shadow of Wisam coming across to her mattress in the night, and the frustrated anger of Umm Wisam as she screamed and complained and ordered her around. She made a decision not to look back. And her legend faded slowly, like some old tale that never attracted the attention of an illustrator.

The Metamorphosis of Said

He helped his father, the grocer Abu Said, after school and at
weekends. He had been an adolescent when he used to help us
carry the brown bags of shopping up to our flat. I remember
his big, ingenuous smile when he'd managed to carry three
water melons to our neighbour upstairs, who always bought
food as if she was preparing for a feast. His presence was
essential for the good of his father's business. The reason for
this was that many people in our neighbourhood thought it
somehow improper to buy food in moderate quantities. Arab
hospitality and generosity have a way of expressing themselves
in the quantities of food left over after dinners and lunches. As
a result, shopping bags were very heavy, and Abu Said, with his
pen stuck characteristically behind his ear, just couldn't cope
on his own any more. He had to help his customers choose the
best of his produce, calculate the bill out loud, make sure that
nobody was being ignored or made to wait too long, and at
the same time compete with the new grocer on the other side
of the street, who had a flashing sign over his door and
employed a full-time delivery boy.

Said was in secondary school, and was doing well. 'Soon he
may go to the *Ecole Hôtelière*,' his father would tell his customers
proudly. There was a great future for those who worked in the

hotel and catering business in Lebanon. That was before the war broke out. Said was a very familiar face, cheerful and sweet, in my neighbourhood before the war. Being the son of the grocer he always refused a tip when he came loaded with the bags of fruits and vegetables that we had ordered by phone. We would ask him about his grades, and he would tell us about his maths teacher, or ask us to help him with some seventeenth-century French text that he'd been given to study for his homework. Nadia, the manicure lady, had acquired a car, a small Fiat, and she had trouble parking it. Said would rush to help her with advice on how best to fit it onto the car-packed pavements. When she was in real trouble, he would take her keys and park it for her. Like many males of his age, he already knew how to drive before he was of an age for a licence. When he was late with the Sunday delivery, all the women in the building would panic. But they all forgave him when he showed up, because his polite, hurried, innocent looks told that he had been busy. Many women in the neighbourhood had already spoken to their husbands about Abu Said's son – suggesting that he might soon need a word placed here or there in order to get his school fees reduced, or that they might check if they knew anyone influential who could help this nice, hard-working boy to train as a part-timer in a hotel or restaurant when he started studying at the *Ecole Hôtelière*.

I find it hard to recall my neighbourhood without also thinking of Abu Said's little shop, the small square room that seemed magically able to provide all the goods you could ever think of. The colourful vegetable stands on the pavement next to his door were a landmark for me. They always gave me this relaxed feeling of familiarity when I arrived home. Inside the cluttered, disorganized and overcrowded shop there was always hope that you might find what you had come for. When Abu Said was too busy, he would tell his son: 'I'm sure if you search under those boxes, you'll find what the lady wants.' And Said would almost always find it, and would hand it to you with a gesture of generosity and an obvious look of pleasure.

It was difficult to think of the name Said separately from the young, helpful face of the grocer's son. But things changed. Just a few weeks after the war broke out. Said was no longer to be seen near his father. Anyway, the grocer hardly even opened the shop any more, because it was too exposed, and few people felt secure coming to it – even when there was a respite in the shelling, or when the snipers had gone to bed. But on rare occasions Abu Said did arrive with fresh vegetables and fruits, and he sold them inside his shop, away from the unsheltered pavement, in those early days of the war. And when loyal customers inquired about Said he would tell them (with a pride that seemed hesitant, for it came just from his lips, and not from his fully expanded lungs, as when he used to boast about his son's achievements in school): 'Said has joined the fighters!'

Soon the name of Said took on an important new connotation. 'Said is ruthless,' you would hear a neighbour saying. 'Said is restless. He's organizing the young men. During the day he teaches them how to attack and at night he's a sniper.' Said is the person that people call when they're trying to find out about somebody who's been kidnapped. Some disagreed over what his behaviour meant: 'He is a true fighter.' 'No he's just been getting rich from stealing with his militia.' 'If your car's been stolen, try Said, it's probably with one of his men.'

When the war reached its ultimate horror, people claimed that Said had been the driver of the car by which the body of a victim from 'the other side' had been dragged through the streets of the neighbourhood. 'Said is a torturer.' So said the less terrorized inhabitants of the street where we lived. The young and smiling Said was now never seen. Instead he was now imagined in the most frightening terms. Said had been turned by the war into a small monster. He should have been suavely and efficiently managing a little hotel by now, somewhere in one of the famous tourist and holiday resorts that the Lebanese were once so proud of. Both these Saids are real. I have seen many of them. Too many of them. Both before and after the civil war. I have seen their bright hopeful faces, and I have seen them ready to kill and torture. Sticking their Kalashnikov in your face at some checkpoint, like hunters looking for a species that they've suddenly decided to eliminate from the environment. Who is to decide, now, who the real Said is – the Said who might be judged, now that everything is settling back into 'normality'? Where did Said create and store all the cruelty that made him so feared and famous?

Last year, when I went back home, I noticed that Abu Said's shop was once again brightening the pavement with its fresh fruit and vegetables. Instead of the old feeling of security and familiarity, a sort of anguish took hold of me. What if Said was inside? What if I met him? Would I greet him with the same words that I used before? Would I look into his face and search for signs of cruelty in his eyes? Would he still smile as innocently as he had before? Could we all start again, as if we had had a bad night and were leaving its horrible nightmares behind?

I crossed the street and walked on the opposite pavement. I was afraid to face Said. A sense of resignation, or defeat and tiredness, weakened my legs. Who knows . . .? If war crime tribunals had been set up in Lebanon, might Said and his like had been tried for their horrific deeds? Would I have felt more secure today? Would my legs have carried me more surely past the front door of Abu Said's grocery?

Back in London, in the safety of my flat, in a house that looks like all the others on the street, I conjure up Said the militiaman in my mind's eye. The perfectly symmetrical trees lining the pavement provide me with the necessary boring-cum-reassuring feeling that makes Said a fading reality. For me he is now like a character in a TV movie. I can watch. Or switch off. Or follow in detail as he meets his fellow fighters in some lurid street in the hotel district of Beirut, preparing to face death, indulging in horrible actions and violent orgies of laughter. I can play with his appearance at my leisure, deepen the darkness of his eyes, make his features innocent and charmingly Oriental, or horrible, revengeful and bloodthirsty. All according to my own fears, my selective memories . . . and my own ability to face the unacceptable reality that the line that separates the criminal from the next-door neighbour, the helpful lad from the torturer, is not as clear as I had always thought before the civil war. So many things are becoming less and less clear for me, Mrs Nomy. The line between the good and the bad gets much more blurred when you are no longer a *jeune fille*. In my mind, Said keeps on crossing this line. Back and forth and back again. He drives me dizzy as the flashbacks recur in my mind.

Scene One: Said is not yet a criminal, his smile is still warm and childlike. For the past ten days he has not been able to go to college. All the roads are dangerous. Anyway, the college is closed. His father opens the shop for a maximum of an hour a day because the shelling has been continuous, and his vegetable stands are almost empty. Whenever his father crosses the street, rushing towards his shop, he looks like a prisoner on the run. He checks to see that no mortar, bullet or other flying object is coming his way. He shrinks his body to make it look even smaller than it is. His head retreats inside his shoulders, as if he is expecting a reprimand of some sort, and this infuriates Said, for he has often seen his father bending with humility in front of rich customers. His family seems so powerless. His mother repeats incessantly: What would happen to her and the children if Abu Said died on his way to the shop? She gives up getting dressed each day. Wearing only a faded brown nightgown. Praying and fearing and getting poorer by the day.

Then came a point when Said could no longer stand his mother's complaints. His father didn't really need his help in the shop. Said needed to get out of the tiny flat. To move. To do something. He was sick of the stories of people being killed in their flats while they were sleeping, eating, watching TV. His hatred for the other side, the enemy across the green line, was becoming unbearable. He wanted to silence their shells, to catch their snipers, to frighten them and humiliate them in the same way that they were humiliating his father, destroying his mother, turning her into a hysterical, depressive woman.

He does not do much. After taking some water up the stairs for his mother so that she can cook and so that they can take their baths upstairs, he takes his little transistor radio, listens to the same songs being played over and over again on the local station, and goes out on the balcony – despite his mother's warnings and lamentations – and there he watches the group of militiamen who have settled in at the entrance of the building facing his. They have all that he does not. And they are free of all that he has. The sad, heavy, constant presence of his parents worrying about him. Asking him to hide and to keep a low profile, to smile, like his father, at every potential customer on the street. The militiamen are dressed in a relaxed but manly way. They sit on their chairs with their heads slightly tilted back, their feet stretched way in front; cigarettes hanging constantly from the corners of their mouths, they smoke and laugh and play cards just there on the pavement, next to the door of the building. When a jeep stops with a great sudden screech of its brakes, two lithe and powerful young men jump out of it, adjust the position of their Kalashnikovs on their shoulder and give big, generous handshakes to each one of the militiamen that Said sees from his balcony. To Said these men are beautiful. The glamour that emanates from them fills his heart with dreams. He would like to belong to these men, to be as attractive as they are, to feel as young and powerful as they feel, instead of rotting in this miserable little apartment.

Scene Two: Said is standing with his left foot resting on the wall adjacent to the entrance of the building facing his own. A Kalashnikov next to him leans against the same wall; a cigarette hangs from the corner of his mouth. He is waiting for the jeep to come and collect him. He knows how to jump in quickly, into the front seat next to the driver. He has told his mother, who had tried to stop him from going out, hanging on to his sleeve and begging him not to join the fighters, to keep away from the front door of the building, otherwise he would leave his parents' flat and they would never see him again. He chain-smokes now. Cigarettes are plentiful and free.

He goes into battles and into bars with his fellow fighters. They are courageous and aggressive, feared and courted throughout the neighbourhood. They would never let him down if he was in danger and he would rather die than lose their esteem of his loyalty and bravery. He rejoices in the fear that his Kalashnikov puts in the eyes of passers-by. The blood rushes deliciously through his veins when other cars give way to the jeep he occupies. Nowadays he no longer has to queue. Yesterday he noticed how Mr Rafiq, the haughty customer who always prompted big smiles on his father's face whenever he stepped into the shop, moved to one side to allow Said and his fellow fighters to jump the queue at the bakery. Said could see and feel the fear in Mr Rafiq's eyes. Now Mr Rafiq's daughter, the young and feline Salwa, comes and asks Said to fetch the bread for her family. She uses all her charm and has to hide the humiliation of it, for she has to ask this favour in front of all Said's friends. She pretends not to notice their self-satisfied male expressions as she stands speaking to Said at the door of the building. Said indulges himself in creating situations where people will smile to gratify him in the same way that his father used to smile to gratify his customers. His anger at his father's constant humility is never appeased. Humiliating others and watching how they fear him is endlessly exhilarating.

Then there was that terrible night when one could not tell

stars from missiles. The night when people tucked their faces into their bodies, in order not to hear and not to see. The night that Said and his fellow fighters decided to take their revenge for the death of one of their commanders. People heard their victims screaming, begging. They woke up to the sight of blood in the middle of the streets, and the smell of dying fires and bullets. Children told parents that they were shown ears that had been collected and exhibited by the fighters. Said was leading the fighters and telling them to show no mercy, said the baker, who never closed his business despite all the bombs and the shortages. The name Said was uttered with fear now. Leila, the wife of the barber, swears by God that his eyes had turned red and his hair had grown as long as her arm. Said is a killer, a hero, or a thief, depending on who is telling the story, depending on their fears and needs. For the women who used to love his innocent, childlike smile, Said has now become a symbol of violence and ruthlessness.

I wish I had the courage to get close to Said now, and study his face closely. Would I be able to tell from his eyes if he really had cut people into pieces? Had he maybe just gone mad for a while, when the skies and the city and the earth were shaking and the missiles and bullets and bombs were flying? Now that the noises have faded, will he be back there, behind the counter of his father's shop, ready again to tuck his pen behind his ear, and to teach his own children how to behave properly and smile at customers? When I have the courage to step into Said's shop and greet him politely I will be ready to say that forgiving and forgetting is what we should be calling for. Until then, I will think of you, Mrs Nomy. I will think of your lesson, and face my fears.

Kirsten's Power

I have always cherished the anonymity of hotel rooms. In their square bastions of similarity, their depersonalised and serviced rooms, my isolation fills me with a sense of soothing detachment and something easily approaching serenity. My solitude in a hotel room has always had a taste of victory – a little triumph over my upbringing in a small city in which women were always under scrutiny. Here in these bland, neutral spaces, shielded by their frilled satin curtains and their half-hearted attempts at elegance, I can indulge in unspoken feelings of freedom, a comfortable and ephemeral illusion of independence. But on that fateful evening of 1989 I deeply resented the large empty bed and the dim lights that seemed to weigh so heavily on the room. This time my hotel room felt more like a sedate jail than a sanctuary of tranquillity.

Copenhagen looked sombre and gloomy, and I was feeling sad. Sad like an orphan on a cold, bright, sparkling Christmas day. He was dead. He had been killed. And all I could remember was his broad, playful smile, his enthusiastic curiosity and his impatient, eager pace. His assassins did not care for smiles. It did not matter to them that he was young and full of humour, and that he had friends who would miss him desperately.

Assassins aren't usually concerned about such things. They killed him, and there I was, back in that city of pink and purple memories of quiet bicycles and unpretentious beauty, staring into darkness and seeing only desolation. The streets of Copenhagen stretched bleak and gloomy as I watched through the blurred, wet windows of the taxi that picked me up at the airport. Where were all the colours and the cheerful images that had so enchanted me the last time I was here? It was just over a year ago. I had come to visit him and meet his wife Kirsten.

From the day I first met Hashem in Beirut – one refugee among a thousand others who had fled their countries looking for a safe haven on the Mediterranean – we became close friends. But Beirut would no longer be safe for an Iranian dissident, so Hashem went looking for refuge elsewhere. Just as you did, many years ago, Mrs Nomy, he sought refuge far away from the city where both you and I grew up. He ended up in Denmark and there he settled and quickly fell in love with the very good Kirsten. She was wonderful for him. She made him feel at home in this so very different city. She adapted easily to his friends, and she fought tooth and nail with the Danish immigration authorities to bring his brothers and their families to join him in Copenhagen.

His friends envied him. Kirsten was a woman who could soothe their worries and solve the multitude of problems they all faced. She cooked meals that reminded them of their mothers, and what's more she had the looks of an angel. Kirsten looked like one of those unattainable blonde girls depicted in the English-teaching schoolbooks that he must have read when he was a child. Kirsten was too good, and Hashem was so overwhelmed by her kindness that he once wrote me a distressing letter in which he expressed his fear of being eternally indebted to her and her generosity.'It is difficult for a man to accept to be always on the receiving end,' he wrote. He also proudly informed me that she had even proclaimed her willingness to wear the veil if they ever went back to live in his country.

As I read his letter, I realised that he hadn't changed much. He was teasing me about his luck in having found her. Hashem had never really accepted what he described as my 'inauthentic' feminism. He used to say that I'd been influenced by the Western values that had invaded my city and my group of friends. The more I read his catalogue of praise for Kirsten, the more I realised how much Hashem was missing his country, and also how much Kirsten idealized the 'Third World'. She obviously loved the Third World, and it seemed that Hashem was her way of gaining herself access to it.

I felt ashamed of myself – of my thoughts and my sarcasm. The silence of my hotel room was stifling and I was obviously misplacing my anger. The truth was that I was fed up with the sweet smiles that appeared on the faces of good-hearted Western liberals and leftists when they found out where you'd come from, and 'what you must have gone through'. I found myself always wanting to tell them about the fun we had too, and the nastinesses we can be capable of, just like anybody else on this planet. Kirsten was one of those people who made me want to scream these things out loud. Yes, I'd been irritated by her goodness from the very first day I'd visited them in their tidy home in this northern city. It took me less than an afternoon to understand why Hashem's letters, for all their praise of his wife's virtues, seemed to suppress a subtext which spelled out stress and alarm. The fact was, the man was a prisoner of her abiding kindness and her relentless care. Poor Hashem, he could not even admit his own unease to himself. He was, above all else, a very decent person.

The phone rang, cutting abruptly through the silence of my satin room and the desolation of my recollections. It was Kirsten. Her voice at the other end of the line was high-pitched and rapid. She inquired about my trip and the comfort of the hotel she had booked for me. She informed me, with the same rapid efficiency, that the funeral ceremonies would start at 10.00 am the following day. 'If you don't have a black dress, I can lend you one,' she said. 'We will start with a meeting at the town hall, during which leading personalities will pay their respects to Hashem and deliver speeches. I shall give a speech myself,' she added. 'Then we will pray in the church, for my parents' sake, before we go to the mosque for the funeral ceremony. If you need anything, at any time, you can call me. I won't be sleeping tonight.' She hung up before I could say anything. I could not find one right word to express my sympathy for her loss. My hand seemed to be alien to my body as it put down the receiver. Now my room was more like an ugly cube in which I was condemned to spend a long, mute and desolate night. The energy in Kirsten's voice had plunged me into a paralysing passivity.

Did Kirsten know that Hashem had told me about his affair with Maria, and the problems that their marriage was going through? Did it make any difference now that he was to be referred to in the past tense?

What about the other woman, Maria? Would I see her too the next day?

'She's like one of us,' he had told me while we were walking across the Nyhaven. The absolute blue of the sky contrasted joyously with the brightly-coloured frontages of the buildings on either side of the canal. We walked in a feast of yellow-ochre walls and Indian-red roofs, enjoying the nautical flavour of this old sailors' street. Hashem was eager to release his thoughts. He kept walking and speaking, oblivious of the many inviting cafes where we could have sat. Hashem was in love with Maria, a Chilean refugee who was attending the same Danish language course as him. 'She dresses in very colourful dresses . . . likes to eat sandwiches as she walks down the street . . . she understands exactly how I feel. We laugh a lot together . . . I feel incredibly guilty towards Kirsten. I've tried many times to end my relationship with Maria, but I've never succeeded. I need her next to me. I long for her, and I become happy and alive whenever she's around. Kirsten keeps saying that she understands, but I know she's unhappy. She isn't sleeping well, she's always edgy and tense, she watches me all the time. I feel torn. I despise myself for the pleasure Maria gives me, for the suffering I am inflicting on Kirsten. I wish she would hate me, kick me out, blame me. But all she does is stare at me with her big sad brown eyes. They always seem to be telling me: "Look at what you have given me in return for all the sacrifices I made for all the help that I've given you and your family".' Hashem kept asking me what he should do. And I knew better than to give him an answer. There obviously was no answer, and

Hashem went on loving his wife, being in love with Maria, and being simultaneously both happy and miserable. His life went on like that until a few days before my arrival, when he was shot ... when he was left with no choice between happiness or misery ... when the people who drove him out of his country decided that he should no longer exist, no longer speak, no longer write against their prisons, their beliefs, their despotism.

And here I am stuck in a neon-lit nightmare, restless and sleepless in a city that lost all its gaiety this evening, waiting endlessly for the morning to come, for the dawn light to filter through those thick, pink curtains. Harassed and consumed by the same fear and always returning to the same question, like a scratched record: 'Is there no end to our predicament? No place immune to the mess and misery that we have inherited from the past?'

I was not exactly enchanted by either Kirsten's generosity or her austerity. She managed, without ever saying a word, to make me feel guilty about every aspect of my behaviour. When she was around I had a feeling that my make-up was overdone, or my clothes too showy. Worst of all I knew that for her I had to be good, since I was from the Third World. Therefore she would not only tolerate me, but would actively like me. With her I felt like a specimen. And feeling like a specimen does not serve your ego right, believe me. But how can you explain this to nice people like Kirsten? After a week of this kind of generous treatment, I decided that Kirsten could not really be so good or so loving either. Not all the time and not to all of us. I felt that she had to be taking it out on somebody or something, sometime or somewhere. And then I was promptly ridden with guilt for feeling such a thing. She had managed to make me feel lousy and mean, and angry at myself for being insensitive to virtue and goodness.

Hashem, being a man, had no problem being liked and adored. He indulged in anti-Western phraseology, and this made him something of a hit among Kirsten's friends in Denmark. He had little left but his status of political refugee and his popularity, and he was missing his country, his noisy street and the familiarity of his mother-tongue. But to be fair to him, he managed to hold on to his best features: his alert curiosity and the lightness that created fun and humour around him. I related to this lightness and I understood his need for success. It was all he had left in this very different city and this never-ending exile. Maria was sweet, wasn't much of a one for health and ecology, never tried to dissuade him from smoking like a chimney, and liked only herself and him.

We never agreed on anything much, Hashem and me, but we enjoyed each other's company and we developed a kind of stubborn solidarity. We savoured this little tacit, teasing attitude towards each other, and we settled into our role as accomplices of a sort. He was afraid of my getting too integrated into the West. 'Beyond the point of no return.' I, on the other hand, would scream at him for his endless need to prove that 'the East is more human and less calculating than the West'. A common past was what united us, along with a capacity not to take ourselves and our disagreements too seriously. Even now, at this late hour of this eternal empty night, I found myself arguing with him in my head: 'Hashem, honestly ... If you had been assassinated in your own country, do you think that I, as a woman, could have come on my own, as simply as this, to stay in a hotel room in order to attend your funeral the following day?' I realised that his answer would never come, and suddenly I found myself missing him terribly.

I was the first and only person in the lobby of the hotel waiting for morning coffee to be served. Hashem's picture was on the front pages of the newspapers, but I had no clue what they were saying about either him or his killers. They all had printed the same picture, a picture in which he looked very respectable. They seemed to be on his side, but what did that matter now that he could neither win nor lose anything?

I was saved from map-reading my way across Copenhagen to attend the ceremony. Kirsten had organised everything and thought of every little detail. A taxi was sent to collect me from my hotel. The driver solemnly handed me a navy-blue scarf that Kirsten had wrapped in a package with my name on the front. I realised that many of the other women had been given similar scarves when I arrived in the taxi at the imposing building, where a small crowd had gathered. Kirsten came across to me immediately. She moved swiftly and purposefully, her face showing determination. Her movements conveyed a sense of purpose. Her black dress stood out powerfully in the midst of the silent crowd. As if it was a dividing marker between the low, grey sky, and the morose grey pavement.

Kirsten came towards me. She thanked me for coming and showed me where I was to stand. Then she moved on to direct another person to the front of the gathering, at the entrance where the podium had been placed. Kirsten had the movements and gestures of a busy hostess ensuring that her guests were properly taken care of. A disturbing liveliness emanated from her eyes. She was overflowing with energy. Suddenly a microphone was handed to her and her voice, clear and strong, attracted all attention towards the podium where she was now standing. She was reading a poem she had written in English for Hashem. I was hearing her voice, but I felt unable to listen. The whole setting brought back to me the reality of Hashem's death. It hit me like a soundless slap in the face, weakening my knees and affecting me in my gut. Phrases and words – not meanings – reached me from Kirsten's lips. She was going to 'continue his mission'. Words like comrade and husband and promise came through to me as if they were made of their own echoes. Kirsten ended her speech pronouncing what seemed to be a pledge that she delivered in Persian. My vision of her was blurred, my hearing was somehow numb, and I could not tell if this was the result of disgust or admiration. I was terrified by the disagreeable thought that I might actually faint in the midst of all this assembly.

I took a deep breath and dragged myself away from the crowd. I needed to see the river, to make sure that it was still there, that its waters were still blue and that its pretty boats hadn't turned grey. As I was leaving, I noticed the ravaged face of Maria, who was relegated to a very remote corner of the proceedings. She was standing there like a distant relative whose own sufferings did not need to be taken into account. She had lost him, but was not allowed to share her grief openly with others who had loved him. I stopped and walked back towards her. I needed to kiss her and comfort her and tell her that I knew how much Hashem had loved her. I had a strong feeling that Kirsten was staring at me furiously. It was a feeling. I did not dare look towards the podium where she was standing. A feeling of guilt and a sense of relief took hold of me as I hugged Maria – I really wish I'd had the opportunity to hug you before you left us Mrs Nomy . . . Now I was free to distance myself from Kirsten's ceremony, to breathe a bit of fresh air. I dreaded the wide spaces of the city's streets. I felt a desperate need to reach my square, cushioned room back at the hotel.

News of Kirsten continued to reach me through the numerous activities that she organised to keep Hashem's memory and his mission alive. Kirsten, I was told, had dedicated her life to Hashem's memory. 'She is such a faithful, devoted woman. She's even given up practising law,' I was told by a mutual acquaintance who had seen her during a trip he made to Copenhagen. I never heard from Maria.

Kirsten had succeeded in erasing her from Hashem's posthumous existence. Hashem was all hers now. Now that he was dead, she could do with him whatever she liked. She was in full and absolute control, for now he was hers and hers alone. She was still taking her revenge over the frustrations that she had endured so willingly while he was alive. I have never been to Copenhagen since. I could not envisage either seeing her or not seeing her, if I had gone.

I find I can no longer quietly savour the ordinary anonymity of a hotel room. Hotel rooms have a taste of stale revenge and silent rage. They are inhabited by Kirsten's voice and tense smile, and they leave no place for your advising/teaching voice, Mrs Nomy.

On Being Judged

On the wall behind my bed a graffiti survives, unaffected by the damage done by the shelling. Angular words in red declare bluntly on a wall that is less than white: '*Les moralisateurs sont des insolents et des hypocrites.*'

I couldn't bring myself to paint my bedroom wall during my last visit. Much as I hate slogans of any kind nowadays, I wanted to leave this graffiti that had survived so much. We children of the sixties loved such phrases: they felt generous and, more importantly, they sounded liberated. We hated to think of ourselves as sounding judgmental, let alone *being* judgmental. The worst insult we could hurl at somebody was that they were 'self-righteous'. And the most shameful feeling was when we felt that this accusation, when directed at us, carried some truth. And how could there be no truth in such accusations? After all, we are human and cannot survive without judgements. The best we can hope is that they are kept to a minimum, and that they are not always entirely based on prejudices.

We still like to think of ourselves as not opinionated, even when passing opinions on justice versus injustice, fairness versus unfairness, or maybe just on which is the best film in town. This is why, after having fought the 'battles of the sixties' and adored Pasolini's films and Allen Ginsberg's poems and the lifestyle of Simone de Beauvoir and Jean-Paul Sartre, postmodernism appeared to be our saviour. We could have opinions and support causes while at the same time claiming that they were not purely Just Causes, but personal inclinations and choices. Our own relative values. As in shopping, so in ethics – feel free to pick and choose.

All this seems possible until something happens. Like the mass cold-blooded rape of hundreds of Bosnian women. Like the fire bomb thrown into the house of an Asian family by an over-excited white racist in east London, which resulted in the death of a mother and her five children. Like the slaughter perpetrated, maybe with axes or maybe with guns, by a white gang or a black gang which is not benefiting from the recent anti-apartheid measures in South Africa. Or like one family in France and another in London, who defy the law and hold down a four-year-old girl by force and make her lie naked on the floor in order to cut her clitoris with sharpened scissors for the sake of family honour and tradition.

This is when you find yourself passing opinions and holding forth about what is right and what is wrong. This is when you want the family of the little four-year-old to be punished. This is when you do not care about cultural relativism but dream of one thing and one thing only – to save this little victim from the self-righteous torture that her family is inflicting on her. You want to call the police to bring their 'Western law' to stop the parents. You utter words of anger. You feel disgust. You long for the parents to have to go through the same hell that their daughter has endured. This is when you have to face the fact that actions have to be related to their consequences. And that the business of pardon, forgiveness, blame and punishment is not to be left to those who confuse it with revenge.

Listen to this, Mrs Nomy, because this concerns us very directly – you as a teacher and me who is writing all this because of you. Wherever you are now living, do you still read, as I do, French magazines? After all, you are the one responsible for our inability to escape French language and French culture. Did you happen to read the complaint by the French philosophy teacher entitled 'The Perverse Consequences of Tolerance' in *Le Nouvel Observateur*, 6–12 July 1995, where he talked of his students' total lack of desire to pass judgement? He had been marking the papers of 200-odd baccalaureate students, who had been asked to write an essay on the theme of 'Can we justify everything?' He had been struck by the fact that almost all the students gave what he called strange answers. With very few exceptions, all thought that Hitler had fought for something which he believed just, and that if one lived in a different context, if one could look at things from Hitler's point of view, then it became difficult to judge him. Nine out of ten of the essays tried to explain that, *grosso modo*, we could and should understand everything.

The professor was terrified by what he called the deadly relativism that was taking hold of the young generation. 'We have been engulfed by the sovereign religion of tolerance and we have raised children who find it difficult to differentiate between values and beliefs, between opinions and truths. Justice, impartiality, neutrality and indifference are nearly the same thing. Aesthetic tastes cannot be discussed either; only with great difficulty will they accept the idea that there is such a thing as ugly and such a thing as beautiful. It is forbidden to

judge! I think we should all start to question ourselves on this
spirit of our times, which is leading our youth to be incapable
of thinking and of having dialogue with others.'

The professor's article made me uneasy with my over-
enthusiastic point of view about non-judgmentalism – an
enthusiasm that grew out of my experience of the civil war in
Lebanon and its hellish fanaticism – its readiness to label people
according to their religion, their beliefs or their national origin,
and once this rigid label was made to stick, to do with its wearer
what one does with merchandise: adopt it, reject it, or tear it
into pieces if it's faulty. I understood better a phrase that Vaclav
Havel, the person whom I most admired of all modern
statesmen, once said. It had really annoyed me when I first read
it. 'Notions such as justice, honour and betrayal possess in this
world a content that is very concrete.'

I will never forget the terrible afternoon when I saw a group
of men, in Nabaa, a poor neighbourhood near Tell el-Zaatar
camp on the outskirts of Beirut, trying to haul a young woman
away from the door of a militia centre. She was not easy to
tame. In her hand she was holding a hammer, and she would
not let go of it. I was told that she had gone into the centre, and
had begun to rain hammer blows on a young prisoner from
the opposite camp. Her brother had died in the fighting the
previous day, and she was coming to take her revenge on one
of 'them' – one of those from the other side responsible for the
death of her brother. The prisoner may die from her vicious
blows, they told me. She would not stop, they said.

I walked away, nauseated. I still cannot forget her terrible,
distorted features, her wrathful eyes, her wild, disconnected
gestures. They recur in my memory like a badly programmed

video. She could not comprehend why her own side was acting as if she was not within her rights. The more her obvious 'truth' was challenged, the more her gestures seemed disconnected. What was it that made a woman act in this horrible manner? Is it permissible for us to condemn her with values that are alien to her? I always wonder whether they would have let her go ahead with her bloody and hysterical revenge if she had been a man instead. Did they try to stop her because she was acting as a 'hysterical woman'? In a way she looked like one of the witches that filled our childhood nightmares: dishevelled, her face red and ugly with fury, her hands splayed like an octopus around the hammer. We know today that witches were victims, and the haunting memory of this woman disturbs me as a woman. Since I saw her eagerness to spill blood and to kill, I find it harder to say things like: 'Women don't need war, they don't have penises to project in the way that men do', or 'We have our periods and men are envious – they want to be able to bleed and spill blood too'.

For the last three days I have been obsessed by images from a film, *Farewell My Concubine*. Images of success, greed, sensuality, all in scarlet and gold. But most of all, the story of punishment. Both 'deserved' and 'undeserved'. Punishment deriving from a haunting need to cleanse and start again from a point-zero of memory, or punishment to satisfy the need for revenge in the new victors. At first it was the images that kept me awake, but then came questions, of increasing complexity. Is the old Teacher-Master really despicable? In one way yes: he is a torturer, he hits children and makes them bleed with his whip for the sake of art and perfection. In another way no: he was pursuing his profession in the way that he understood it, a method inherited through centuries of tradition. His student victims even come back to him after they become famous and successful, to show gratitude and respect. They have internalised his values and end up like him, ready to be torturers themselves for the sake of perfection in art. Or are they perhaps telling us that compassion is not a basis on which to build a future – not when ambitions are too big, and definitely not in a totalitarian society?

Is cruelty a relative value? I find such an axiom hard to digest. I am sure that you do too, Mrs Nomy. However valuable the category of Oriental despotic society may be to analysis, people from those societies themselves have revolted against despotism and cruelty. The film-maker of *Farewell My Concubine* is Chinese. In the best tragic tradition he depicts the dilemma of a frightened, weakened person who ends up 'betraying' the person he loved most before the accusing masses of the Cultural Revolution. He, in turn, is betrayed by the person who owes him his life. The circle of accusation, betrayal, revenge, fears and 'cowardly' behaviour is dramatised in a way that would be recognizable to a witness of the McCarthyite trials in the US, by a citizen of Athens some thousands of years ago, or by any citizen of Baghdad in the last thirty years. There may be more or less blood – and that is important – and there may be more or less subtlety but the expression on the faces of the protagonists would reflect the same dilemmas of the human condition.

I am terrified by the idea that you might find this world more complicated than you thought when you explained it to us.

Noha's Quest and the Passion of Flora

'*I am the martyr Noha Samman. When you watch me and hear my words, I will not be on this earth any more. I will have joined the heroes and the glorious combatants who gave their blood before me for our sacred cause. I am not the first martyr for our great struggle and I know that I shall not be the last. I shall die in an explosion that will shine with a fire in which dozens of our enemies will burn. My death will glow in a feast of light that will allow no traitor and no coward to show their faces in our land ever again.*'

Her face is passionate and her voice limpid. They come through the TV screen on this hot August evening, and they silence us. Noha, the 16-year-old woman, the lively adolescent, blew herself up this afternoon. We witness with fear and silence the ritualised preparations for her death. She had filmed a video for us to see, for her message never to be forgotten, and for her face to inhabit our nightmares. Somehow the sounds of shells and bombs seem to have receded into a hush and Beirut is invaded by one single sound: the voice of a pretty young girl speaking from a TV screen. The dead brought back to life.

Beirut had been noisily debating the suicide attack that

killed dozens of people in the South that afternoon. Some maintained firmly that the number of the enemy who had perished was in the hundreds. Others ventured nervously to disagree with such methods of resistance. A man claimed that he had heard the sound of the explosion in his home in the southern suburb, and that the blast had knocked things off his kitchen shelves. The stories were exchanged, the rumours were transmitted, and the opinions expressed were agreed with or disagreed with in the loudest and noisiest way until the grave voice of a TV broadcaster announced the big surprise. 'Noha Samman, a 16-year-old martyr was responsible for today's bomb in which dozens of the enemy perished. We will shortly show the video that she asked us to broadcast to the nation.'

'Forgive me, mother. I know my death will cause you grief. I had no choice. I responded to the need of my country and I had to leave you. Mother, I love you. Be proud of me. Rejoice, for today is the happiest day in my life. Don't think of me as dead, but as an undying symbol of sacrifice and combat against evil. You dreamt of seeing me in a white dress. Look at me. I am wearing the white dress. My virginal blood I offer to my cause, our cause: the best and most honourable suitor. My blood is not mine alone, it belongs to my people.'

A circle of silence, heavier than the August heat, falls on us, and death speaks to us from the little screen through the lips of this woman-child. Her hair is long and black, her mouth tense and determined, and from her eyes shines the passion of the absolute. On the wall behind her hang the portraits of various martyrs. They looked down from the wall as if placed there to give weight to her words. Her tense lips sketch a smile.

Noha is expressing happiness to the camera, like a character in a play. We see only her face, and we listen to her joyful words:

'My mother, my people, don't feel sad. Dance, sing and rejoice in my funeral. Prepare yourself for the feast. This is my wedding day. I have written the word Martyr with my blood on the sheets of my wedding night. I am happy today. I feel alive, for life is in honour, in combat; and death is not what I am going to meet, for death is in resignation and national shame. I am overjoyed. I am looking forward to joining the heroes and the just in Paradise. I am looking forward to feeling the embrace of the land that my spilled blood will water and nourish. I am not dead, I am starting a new life. A life of pride and new beginnings.'

Noha's face fades from the screen, and the silence in the streets is broken by the firing of thousands of bullets, in celebration of her martyrdom. The atmosphere is sadly apocalyptic. Radios all over the neighbourhood compete in playing loud nationalist songs. TV watchers jump channels, seeking more details, more drama. 'Soon we will be going over to our reporter, with Noha's family, to hear the reaction of her parents, and her young sisters and brother. Stay with us.' So says the pretty blonde TV announcers, who looks excited at the prospect of being so much in the middle of things.

Our voyeurism is excited by the blonde reporter who is shown standing outside the door of Noha's home. But we lose patience, and move to another channel hoping to see more, to explore this feast of death from all its angles. On the next channel, a modern nationalist militant dressed in an impeccable western suit is giving his opinion: 'Noha's glorious action is a sign of great hope. This is a sacrifice that announces a bright future. We Arabs are known for our generosity, and we are proud of it. If we have only a little food in our home, we keep it for our guests. The highest generosity is to give one's soul and one's blood to the most welcomed of guests: to dignity, and authenticity, and the glorious revival of our great nation. What is man's greatest virtue and his most cherished quality? Generosity. Noha gave her pure blood and her beautiful youth to what she believed in, to our fight for sovereignty and national pride. Against the enemy and his Western allies. Look at her face – she is beautiful. She did not decide to die because life held nothing for her. She had many suitors dreaming of having her as a wife. She died because she loved her country more than her own life, and because her soul was even more beautiful than her face.'

We return to the blonde TV reporter, and she is interviewing people in the crowd that has gathered around Noha's home. There is a lot of movement near the door. Important political leaders, surrounded by bodyguards and militiamen, come and go from the building where Noha lived. From time to time a voice shouts: 'With our souls, with our blood we will avenge you, oh Noha' and hundreds of voices repeat the phrase in unison while Kalashnikovs are raised and clenched fists wave above the heads of the crowd. The reporter has to raise her voice to ask us to be patient. Soon, she says, she will be talking to Noha's mother. We try a third channel and there, between verses from the Koran and some colourful pictures of the South, a sheikh is telling us about martyrs.

'*The martyr reaches a happiness that the ordinary believer does not know. The believer does not want to kill, for he is on this earth to glorify God. But if he has to die defending his religion then he is a martyr, and he will know all the pleasures of Paradise. No pleasure is higher than that of worshipping God. And if this worship means that the believer should die or kill the enemies of God, so be it, for if death is inevitable, let it be honourable. The martyr's blood is of beautiful red and its smell is that of musk.'*

The sheikh stops, adjusts his position, adopts an authoritative tone and a more solemn posture and then advises:

'Bury the martyr in his clothes. The clothes he was wearing when he died. For he should not be separated from his wounds and his blood. He should meet his God bearing all the marks of his heroic sacrifices. The world exhibits plenty of attractions, it has many wonders that can attract the eye and steal the heart. Money and gold and pretty women, they all play with man's soul and reason. But when the knowledge of God is well rooted in a man's heart, all these attractions turn into ghosts. Ghosts that are despicable. The pleasure of knowing God and worshipping him is the most delectable pleasure ever to be known.'

The sheikh was speaking as if we still lived in the era when martyrs perished with a sword in their hands. And he speaks as a heterosexual man. No trace of Noha would ever be found among the rubble and the fires left by the blast of her car-bomb. But since the sheikh is charismatic and the atmosphere is so loaded with tension, nobody notices such details, for in these moments centuries long-gone are re-emerging in a sudden confusion, like a sleeping volcano that has waited too long to erupt again and now begins spewing out a lava that nothing can stop.

We never saw Noha's mother on our screen, despite the

promises of the ambitious blonde announcer. Later that evening there were reports that Noha's mother had declared her forgiveness of her daughter. What's more, she was very proud of her, and she was preparing candy boxes with pink ribbons for the funeral. It would be a celebration. One well-known patisserie that specialised in wedding cakes placed adverts in the papers, announcing that they were sending a multi-layered wedding cake which would have an icing-sugar heart on top, half in pink for Noha, and the other half in blue, representing her *fiancé*, the South of Lebanon. We never saw Noha's father either, but various newspapers, as well as some political activists, had all heard him say that he would be happy to see Noha's brothers and sisters follow her example. When we saw TV footage of her mother and father walking in the funeral processions, they were not chanting; they walked in silence, looking into nothingness. They were surrounded by prominent party and militia leaders who strained to make themselves more visible to the multitude of cameras that occupied every available space. Behind them marched a noisy demonstration, chanting the two slogans that filled the streets and avenues of Beirut in constant repetition: '*With our souls, with our blood we would pay for you, oh Martyr.*' '*Oh mother of the Martyrs, sing the song of joy; all of us here are your children.*' The human voices had to compete with the endless flow of bullets firing into the air. The bullets celebrating Noha's wedding!

After the funeral a lot of people didn't feel like going home. A few dozen spent the night crying and celebrating Noha's martyrdom around the Martyrs' Fountain, a monument that had been erected a few months previously to glorify the power of spilled blood. A sculpture that left no room for abstraction, it stood in the middle of the square. It contained red-dyed water that moved in a circular motion. The young crowd that gathered around it that night vied with each other to get closer to the fountain, and fought for the privilege of being soaked by its waters. The people who lived near the monument did not dare come too close, but they heard the young people screaming, and were not sure whether the screams were from fear, joy or anger.

A few weeks later the pictures of Noha that had filled the walls of West Beirut had begun to disappear under the pictures of new '*heureux élus*', as all the martyrs were now being called. The 'Happy Elect'. There were many such chosen people in Lebanon then – many men and a few women. Every militia claimed a growing number of dead, a longer litany of martyrs in the list of the war victims. But the photos had to compete for space on the walls and the '*fiancée* of the South' was fast disappearing beneath photos of newcomers. Often you would see her lips, or half her face, still visible under a new photo that had been hurriedly plastered over the top. On one occasion her picture was covered with red-painted slogans that spoke of death, even younger death: Beirut will fall only like great cities fall: after its last child.

Words that kill and spill blood daubed over the faces of all the young martyrs; 'We will trace our route through a sea of blood.' So said a slogan that was painted over Noha's face, completely obliterating her.

Many nationalist poems were dedicated to Noha during the

following month. She was not there to listen to them. In a little
booklet that she had left in her room, she had copied, from the
volumes on her older brother's bookshelf, many poems that
celebrated martyrdom for the cause of the nation. Among them
were some that resembled the ones that were later to be written
for her. In her childish handwriting she underlined the words
of the earlier poets that seem to have marked her most deeply:

Martyrdom is only for him who dies defending a right,
and who does not care what happens to himself . . .
The martyr is he who would pay with his youth for the glory
*   of his nation,*
and whose name is valued only with gold . . .

And she who chooses the grave for a home
will gain a pride that no lived years can match . . .
From the souls of the martyrs, a breeze emanates
enchanting the beautiful places and eternally refreshing the
*   souls of the living.*

    (Khalil Mutran, Lebanese poet who resided in Egypt)

They are not dead,
They are all alive.

The earth and the skies chant their names . . .
the night covers faces and takes them away,

but the souls prevail,
for they are light.

    (Nicholas Fayad, commemorating the deaths of the six
      martyrs killed by Jamal Pasha in Lebanon in 1916)

Darken the lands with victims
When the victims are spread to the horizon
They all become alive

(Yousef al-Khal, Lebanese modernist poet)

In the centre pages of her booklet, with great care, she had copied the poem of Nizar Kabbani, a poet adored by all her girlfriends. It was his famous love poem *Gharnata* (Granada) and around it she had drawn an elegant frame, made of garlands that ended with a different flower at each corner of the page. Kabbani, like many other poets, is expressing his nostalgia for the loss of Andalus. His nostalgia is triggered by a beautiful woman whom he meets in Spain, at the entrance to the Alhambra. In her black eyes he travels back seven centuries. He sees the Umayads' flags flying. She guides him through the wonders of the Alhambra, and she tells him:

This is Alhambra, the pride of our ancestors.
Read my glory on its walls.
Her glory!! I caressed my open wound,
and I caressed a second wound in my heart.
If only my beautiful inheritor knew
that those she is naming are my ancestors

I embraced in her when we separated
a man called Tarek Ibn Ziyad.

The young girl who had copied those words of passion and illustrious memory with such loving care was reaching for an absolute and dreaming of eternity. What she may not have known is that many centuries earlier another very young woman, in the Andalus that had inspired her favourite poet, had given her life in a similar quest, and with the same fervour. Only this time, the young woman was called Flora. Her cause was Christian Spain. And her enemies were the ancestors of whom Noha's poet sings. Listen to the story of Flora, Mrs Nomy.

The *qadi* was fingering his moustache, slowly adjusting it and curling its ends upward. It had been a relaxed day, and soon he would leave the courtroom to join his friends. They would enjoy a glass of wine, and listen to poetry as they nibbled on almonds, dates and raisins. He found the delicate taste of wine far more enjoyable now that Cordoba was drinking it in vessels of fine glass the way they did in Baghdad.

He looked around him with pride and satisfaction. His seat was made of soft leather and the chequered curtains that softened the impact of the sun's rays were made of the best Persian textiles. Thanks to the poet Ziryah and his love for refinement, the people of Cordoba, at least the cultivated and elegant ones like himself, had abandoned their thick silver and golden goblets to drink heavenly sparkling wine from glasses that were delicate and transparent. The *qadi* lifted his perfumed silk robe and walked slowly across the soft carpet towards his desk. He would read a few pages of law before calling it a day.

But he had little opportunity to concentrate. No sooner had he found the page that he had marked the day before when he heard the echoes of terrible screams approaching from behind the damascene door of the courtroom. 'I need to see the *qadi* at once,' said a thin, dishevelled young man, opening the door despite the clerk's objections. With his other hand he was clutching the wrist of a young woman, and he dragged her forcibly behind him. 'You are not my brother, I disown you, I hate you and your religion,' screamed the young woman as she struggled hopelessly to free herself from the man's grip. This was when the *qadi* realised that she could not be more than fifteen or sixteen years of age. Her features were a mesmerizing blend of innocence and determination. The *qadi* made a sign to the clerk indicating that he should let them in.

'*Qadi*, this is my sister Flora. An apostate. A renegade of Islam. The devil invaded her mind and she has converted to Christianity. She deserves to die beheaded and her body should be left to rot for all to witness the enormity of her crime!'

The *qadi* barely had time to digest the man's words when Flora started to scream, in a voice that sounded much older than herself:

'I am a Christian, my mother is a Christian, and I have nothing to do with your prophet and his so-called teachings. Yes I pray to the Virgin Mary, because she is a Saint, and she is pure and because Spain is Christian and was usurped by people like you and this so-called *qadi*. I hate you. Go ahead and kill me, for I don't care for my body. My soul is longing to meet our Saviour. I will go to heaven. You and your religion of lies are afraid of dying because you will all burn in hell. I am a Christian. Try if you dare to take me away from Christ by torture and torment. I am happy to endure them all.'

'Listen to her, *qadi*,' said the brother. 'She is blasphemous, and I cannot bear it any longer. Our father – or rather, mine, for she does not deserve him – died recently, and I am her protector. I ask you to apply the law and have her executed.'

The *qadi* lifted his finger to bid them be silent. He had been taken unawares, and needed a few seconds to assess the situation. This woman must be one of the new zealots that were fighting against Arab rule in Spain. They were a very small minority, a small group of fanatics. People were happy in Cordoba, and the Christians had no real complaints. These fanatics were shouting to the wind. Poor girl – look at her, she is so young, so innocent ...

'Ahem,' said the *qadi*, coughing and adopting an authoritative tone, 'You, Flora, should be severely punished for the miserable words that your lips have uttered. You do not seem to know what you are saying. I forbid you to say one more word in this court. It seems that you are repeating words that you do not even understand, and ...'

'Oh yes I do,' she interrupted. 'I mean every word I said. You are thieves, your religion is that of the devil and your prophet is a false one, an imposter.'

'Execute her at once. My family will not tolerate an enemy of Islam in its midst. We brought her up as a good Moslem, and she learned the Koran and practiced the teachings of our Prophet – God be with him – until the Christians perverted her mind and soul. She thinks Jesus is God, and she practises rites that are despicable. We do not want her among us. She is a disgrace to our family and our religion. *Qadi*, you know better than I do that the penalty for apostasy is death.'

The *qadi* walked towards them, looking angry and severe.

He knew that the girl should be punished, and if the people outside the court had heard this silly woman's terrible insults against the Prophet and his religion he would have had no choice but to sentence her to death. But he was a man praised for being wise and fair, and the city was an example of peace and prosperity. Christian merchants were prospering. Christian functionaries were well paid. Those who did not want to pay the *dhimma* tax could easily convert, and many did. People were free to make their own choices. Thoughts ran through his mind. This woman is acting in the most foolish way, but my heart feels pity for her. She is too young to die, and the last thing I want is to create martyrs for those fanatics.

'Your sister will be punished. She is sentenced to be beaten. Once she has received the lashes she deserves, I will send her back to you. Keep her under good surveillance. Teach her again and again the virtues of our religion. God is merciful. Go now. It is late and the court has to close.'

The *qadi* ordered his clerk to take Flora to her punishment. He felt like being on his own for a while, and realized that he was in no mood to join his friends for reading poetry.

Flora did not stay in her brother's house for long. She ran away soon after, and sought refuge in a convent where she knew she would meet the great Eulogius. When she saw him for the first time she was possessed by every word he said. As he spoke, he tried hard not to look at her. They shared the same faith and the same hatreds. His speech was a revelation. She absorbed every word he spoke. She was carried away by his urgent pleas to his fellow Christians: 'Our strength is in our enthusiasm for sacrifice. Self-denial is the source of peace to the real Christian. The Arabs have perverted our learned men, so that instead of reading the holy scriptures they spend their time trying to acquire the arts of poetry, romance and elegant style. Great Christian minds have abandoned theological commentaries for the so-called delights of contemporary literature. Look at the decadent trappings that the occupiers are bringing into our country, into our simple Christian homes and our modest souls. It is time to save the souls of our fellow Christians. To regain our lost dignity and impose the glory of God and his son Jesus Christ on our land and among our people. We look forward to meeting death and perishing under their torments, for the taste of death will be sweet and the martyrs are saints, for they feast in heaven above us.'

Eulogius felt more inspired and his words became more passionate as he sensed the impact that his preaching was having on the beautiful Flora. Her beauty was nothing but the reflection of the purity of her heart and the nobility of her soul, he told himself. Looking deep into her radiant face, he paused and said: 'Virginity is the flower of the seed of the church. The virgin is the bride of the eternal King, always a spouse, always unwed. The bodies of virgin martyrs are like Christ's temples, and God's spirit dwells within them. The soul of the martyr shines with charity, is sharpened with truth and brandished with the power of a fighting God. Martyrdom is the highest of delights, for it means eternal glory.'

A deep sense of peace took hold of Flora, for now she knew

what her fate would be – the bride of the eternal King and Eulogius's disciple and companion. Her vocation was to die spreading the beautiful words that she had just heard. She, like Eulogius, was burning with love of the truth, the one and only truth, that of the Holy Trinity, and with hatred of all lies and decadent acts. She would speak out loud about them, and throw them in the face of the *qadi* and his likes.

And so she did, despite the warnings issued by Cordoba's council of bishops against fanatical acts of pointless provocation. This time the *qadi* had no choice: Eulogius was attracting a growing number of disciples and Flora was becoming a legend in her lifetime. The khalif, Abdel Rahman, had run out of patience with these zealots who were insulting everything that Moslems held sacred. He had only once choice: to apply the law. Flora was beheaded on a cloudy day in the autumn of 851, along with her companion Mary. Flora's name was later to appear in the list of Christian saints: Saint Flora, the Virgin-Martyr.

Ten centuries apart, the quests of Flora and Noha had a similar taste of dreadful passion, a taste of eternity and blood. Had I not been your student, Mrs Nomy, would I too have taken passion and high principle to a dreadful end? Had I not been your student, would I too have run the risk of confusing my own quest for justice with the sensual elixir of danger? The literature that you taught me to love helped me understand what an overwhelming aphrodisiac the proximity of death can be. I read Georges Bataille after the war. I never approached these things directly, but only through the filter of literature. But now I can look them straight in the eye.

Traitors and Conquerors

'The youth of the poet listens to history through the doors of legends.' So says Victor Hugo, your favourite poet, Mrs Nomy, in his *Légende des Siècles*. The legends narrated to us by the chronicles of al-Andalus, Islamic Spain, are prime material for the extraordinary encounter between Moslems and the West – an encounter that has invaded modern memories and shaped the nostalgia of the Arabs of today, just as it continues to feed Europe's tormented relation with its 'other'.

Many peoples met in Spain and fought over its mountains and groves. Two powerful faiths competed with each other, tolerated each other in good times and clashed in mutual hatred at times of overheated fervour. The splendour of what was known as Arab civilization in Spain is a cry of hope for the Arab poets and the Arab historians of today. That was the era when 'we brought refinement, prosperity and knowledge to the West'. The closeness of this encounter meant endless wars as well as happy and fruitful exchanges. It was an arena for both palace intrigues and absolute loyalties; it bred as many heroes as it manufactured traitors. It exalted intelligence and sophisticated tastes, except when some outburst of religious fanaticism and excess broke through the prevailing wisdom and toleration, spreading blood and making martyrs on the way. In those days heroes and traitors were innumerable, and in a way they were interchangeable, depending on the author of the chronicle concerned, or the period in which their history was recorded. Honourable princes and cowardly governors, heroes and scoundrels, were a daily reality in every province and every street of Moorish Spain, feeding the legends and the moral beliefs of those who go rummaging in history for lessons for today.

Arab civilization was undoubtedly far superior to other civilizations of its days. Arab advances in the fields of philosophy, science and literature were deeply beneficial to Western civilisation. In the end all this collapsed, but it left us with an incredibly rich written legacy. And we could use it in order to do what the poet does in his youth: listen to history through the medium of legend.

We could, for instance, look at the legend of the Conquest of Spain by the Moslems, a legend that mixes righteousness, stirring victories and betrayed loyalties with virginal virtues revenged.

The story of the beautiful virgin Florinda has entered into the mythology of the Arabs as a symbol of Spain's need to be conquered. Florinda, daughter of Julian the governor of Ceuta, was sent by her father, as was the custom among the Princes and Counts of the State, to the court of King Rodrigue, a timorous and ambitious king, in order that she become acquainted with the customs and the etiquette of the aristocracy, and be trained in elegant and refined conduct.

The king was expected to protect these aristocratic young

guests and obviously – in the case of young girls – to defend their honour. But the king seems to have found Florinda irresistible. 'Her golden hair moved gracefully in the silk net that tied her hair, as was the fashion among women in those days. She moved with great elegance, and her long silk clothing revealed a tall, beautiful body as she walked. Her face was round, and her skin so smooth and white that you felt you could almost see through it. Her cheeks were so red and her eyes so blue and clear that they made one think of magic. Her mouth was small and always displayed the most gracious and virtuous smile.' [Girgi Zaydan, *Fath al-Andalus*, Dar Maktabat al-Hayat, Beirut n.d.]

Her beauty had a fatal effect on King Rodrigue. He fell passionately in love with the girl, forgot his promises and responsibilities, and 'usurped Florinda's honour'.

This was an act unworthy of a king – let alone that he already had enough troubles on his hands, with his throne being disputed by the heirs of King Witiza, whom he had deposed, and his kingdom threatened with invasions of Berber troops from North Africa. The lovely and virtuous Florinda managed to send a distressed message to her father, bewailing her lost honour and her miserable fate.

When he read the letter, Julian was filled with anger and rancour. His face turned red with hatred for Rodrigue. He clenched his fists. He screamed with frustration. He now dreamt of one thing and one thing only: to avenge his daughter's honour, and to do as much harm as possible to the unworthy monarch who had been responsible for her downfall. The Arabs are certainly more worthy than this dishonourable man of Spain, thought Julian. He would now give them all the support they needed to invade and conquer; he would show them the way, divulge all the strategic secrets he knew, and even send his best fighters to attack the wretched Rodrigue along with their troops. So it was that Julian was said to have paid a visit to Musa, the son of Noseyr, the Arab governor of North Africa, with whom he had often been at war, and told him that from now on they were allies. When Tarik Ibn al-Walid's troops advanced into Spain, they found they did not have only enemies.

In the view of Arab chronicles and legends Julian acted in an honourable knightly way. However his existence was actually denied by a few Spanish historians of the time who were not prepared to have a traitor among their princes; others maintained that the story of the beautiful Florinda owed more to myth than to reality.

But reality changes, and myths survive, and in Islamic Spain both Christians and Moslems erected monumental heroes such as the Cid, Rodrigo Diaz of Bivar, and Khaled Ibn al-Walid, who pronounced to his soldiers the famous words that left them no choice but to fight: 'The enemy is facing you and the sea is behind you.' These were national heroes who spoke in terms of boldness and conquest, and they have been spared closer scrutiny by their foes as to their respective motivations. Both the Christians and the Moslems wrote ballads and poems that are still recited in schools today, singing the exploits of heroes, blaming traitors and mourning for martyrs. For Arab historians Julian is a virtuous prince and an honourable father; he is much more ambiguous in Christian tales of the *reconquestas*, if he features at all. In some stories Florinda is raped by the king; in others she declares that she would rather die than lose her honour; and in more austere and literary Arab versions she manages to avoid the fatal action of King Rodrigue (always at the last minute), and so becomes an acceptable and untarnished victim who can be allowed into classrooms with young students.

As for the Cid, his legend was continually enhanced, sometimes with conflicting virtues. His sense of honourable conduct was written into a tragedy by Corneille, in which passionate love comes into conflict with the avenging of honour. Rodrigo loves Ximena, but his duty and family pride oblige him to face her father in a duel and kill him. Ximena, his lover, holds the same values as the men of her epoch; her father's death must be avenged, and so she asks Don Sanchez to fight the man she loves. Corneille heightens the drama in the scene in which the Cid, Don Rodrigo, comes to see Ximena before the fatal duel:

> Ximena: *Rodrigo! You! In daylight! Why so bold?*
> *You'll ruin me. Withdraw, I beg of you.*
>
> Don Rodrigo: *I mean to die. Lady, I come to you*
> *Before the fatal blow to say farewell.*
> *The unalterable love I feel for you*
> *Wishes to make you homage of my death.*
>
> Ximena: *You mean to die?*
>
> Ron Rodrigo: *I hasten to the hour*
> *Which will deliver up my life to you.*

Ximena:	You'll die. Don Sancho then can strike such fear
	Into your heart? He's so redoubtable?
	Who has made you so weak and him so strong?
	Rodrigo thinks he's dead before he fights.
	Undaunted by my father or the Moors.
	He goes to fight Don Sancho in despair.
	Thus, then, in direst need, your spirits fail!
Don Rodrigo:	I haste not to the fight but to my end ...
	And even last night the battle had been lost
	Had I been fighting for my cause alone;
	But, in defending King and country, I
	Would have betrayed them with a poor defence.
	My soaring spirit does not hate life so
	As to abandon it, forswearing them.
	Now that my feelings are only at stake,
	I can accept your sentence of my death.
	For your revenge, you chose another's hand
	Since I did not deserve to die by yours ...
Ximena:	... Do not, thus blinded, let yourself forget,
	Just as your life, your glory is at stake,
	and that, whatever Rodrigo's fame in life,
	They'll think him worsted after he is dead.

(Pierre Corneille, *The Cid*, tr. John Cairncross,
Penguin, Harmondsworth, 1975)

The words death, love and honour abound in this tragic encounter. But the violence perpetrated by these lovers is done for the sake of the highest value of their times among persons of their social status: the defence of their reputation. Honour, and the preservation thereof, is viewed only through the eyes of others; it is a duty towards the collectivity, and individuals have to live by its requirements, otherwise the collective – be it clan, tribe or kingdom – would reject them, which is no easy matter in ordinary times, let alone in a world of constant wars. The deeds of our lovers do not belong solely to them. Their doings are to be announced and praised or despised loudly, for there is no such thing as a discreet hero, just as there is no such thing as an anonymous martyr. A martyr would merely be another dead person if his death were to be witnessed discreetly. The 'unknown soldier' is a compromise of modern societies who took their people to wars.

The myth of the Cid is a myth of glory. But glory and heroism are tricky matters, for they are not equally lived by all the parties to the legend. For the Christians who reconquered Spain, the Cid is indeed cast in memories of gilt and bronze. But for the Arab historians, who willingly recognized his courage and military prowess– one chronicle speaks of him as a miracle of God – he was also a ruthless and heartless warrior. The Cid was an ambitious combatant who fought for the Moslem princes as well as for the Christians. As a *chevalier d'industrie* he had been employed to fight for the Moors before their reconquering of Valencia for the Christians, and putting it to fire and destruction. Myo Cid el Campeador, the 'master of single combat', had no problem looting churches as well as mosques in the course of his exploits. Born in 1043, he was a legendary figure, whose fame spread to the four corners of Spain when, having been dismissed by King Alfonso in 1081, he roamed the land seeking his fortune. 'Unburdened by religious or national scruple, he leased his services and those of his men as freely to Moslem princes as to Christian ones, intervening in uprisings whenever he saw an opportunity to acquire loot or power. He showed no scruples as to the means he resorted to [...] An adventurer, who would not hesitate to betray a friend or befriend an enemy [...] He was more of a gang leader than an army commander, roaming through the Eastern Provinces of Spain, ravaging what he found on his way.' In modern times he might have been called a mercenary, but in those days the values of honour and bravery were different and the Spanish Christians desperately needed a champion, a 'miracle of God'. The myth of the Cid tells us to think twice before we go believing in absolute virtue and taking one-sided views of courage and heroism. Corneille, writing in the seventeenth century, was already aware of this contradiction when he made him face Ximena and declare that his reputation and honour were what mattered most, and that as far as love and life were concerned he would be a martyr. Martyrdom, after all, is also a sign of exalted egotism.

In conquering Valencia, Myo Cid the challenger became the stuff of legend. Any scruples he may have had were hard to detect. The Arab poet Abu Ishak Bin Khafaja cried for Valencia, the city that had seen the cruel side of this warrior:

> *The enemies descended on you, wiping away with fire and*
> *desolation your grace.*

Misery passed from hand to hand, faces stared into
  wretchedness,
Looking into what the arms of the night had done to your
  squares.
Homes ceased to be homes and you are no longer yourself.

Like all objects of hero-worship, the Cid could not enjoy fame
without paying a price, for 'honour cannot exist without the
vilification of sanctions'. A hero can only exist in comparison
with cowards, and cowards like heroes could be despised or
ascribed cleverness or sensitivity according to the mood of
the times and the writers of their history. In his famous book
al-Zakhira, Ibn Bassam does not mince words in describing
the Cid – 'this calamity who made every region he entered
famous for its subsequent sadness'– and his deeds. In speaking
of the cruelty of this legendary 'brave warrior', who after
conquering Valencia burned alive most of its notables, Ibn
Bassam wrote: 'The most dog-like of dogs [has been turned]
into a Lion. Called Rodrigo and named the Compreador, El
Cid is a fatal disease that leaves marks of ugliness and hatred
on the Island.'

Arab literature is impregnated with the glorification of
courage. The poet of all Arabs, al-Mutannabi, who lived in the
Abbasid period, wrote endless and unforgettable verses
praising his own heroic courage on the battlefield, as well as
that of the prince to whose court he was attached. His poetry
is so powerful that it is still read by millions even today, for it
reflects values that are as real now as they ever were.

The horses and the nights and the deserts know me
and the swords and the spears and the books and the pens as
*   well . . .*
I am the one whose poetry the blind can see
and whose words can be heard by the deaf
or elsewhere.

Don't believe that glory is a concubine or some wine
Glory is but the sword and fully-fledged victory in battle.

On the other hand, there is a whole string of sayings in Arabic which give an alternative view of this overblown heroism, and give lesser mortals a voice: 'Running away is two thirds of manliness.' And 'a hundred times called coward, and never once called the late.'

The Cid is a hero from another age, an age when men would never be seen crying, and when no man could dare to say 'I am afraid'. He lived at a time when the Christian West needed martyrs and the Moslems were relaxed and more inclined to toleration. Today the roles seem to have been reversed. The Christian martyrs are barely remembered even on the holidays that are linked to their names. Today it is the unhappy Moslem world which is uneasy with itself, whose self-confidence is shaky, and whose discourse is packed with heroes, supermen and martyrs.

The poetry of the modern Arab world abounds with these poems of hurt egos. They are a far (and terrible) cry from the old Arabic saying: 'We have a duty of compassion to the dead.'

The burning fires of Spain
Swallowed in the name of the cross
all sciences and achievements.
Their flames are tongues accusing the soldiers of bad and evil
  to God

So wrote Elias Farhat, in anger, at the beginning of this century.

Suleiman al-Issa, the poet of Arab nationalism, like all elated nationalists of a troubled nation, sings of blood, death and vengeance:

I swear that the tombs will be crowded tomorrow
Crowded with dead people that are not ours
I swear that tomorrow Iraq will explode with revenge
By Abdel Nasser I swear.

Another poet, the Syrian Badawi al-Jabal, speaks of humiliation and of the hatred it generates, a hatred that burned slowly inside him and was alive well into the 1940s when he recited a poem that related to the German invasion of Paris.

I believed in hatred
to feed our will.
I adore God out of pity and weakness.
Woe to the people who did not *darken their red revenge*
with their blood. Blood made of resentment and anger.

. . .

The ultimate generosity is to
water the earth with one's blood while fighting
and to meet one's God thirsty and drained.

. . .

I heard Paris complaining
of her boastful invaders.
Do you remember, now, oh Paris, our complaints?
For twenty years we drank from brim-filled glasses
Overflowing with humiliation.
Get a good taste of humiliation yourself now.
Your greatest men are now servants and collaborators.
Hatred is slowly burning through our wings.
Could not the two of us have avoided all this hatred?

The poet is alarmingly obvious in these lines. Hatred and revenge seep through every word, every letter. But what is most humanly tragic is his last wish. He would have wished to be spared this circle of humiliation, retribution and negative desires.

Should we see Julian and the Cid as betrayers of their people, or were they being loyal to different values when faced with new realities and conditions? Is Badawi al-Jabal disgustingly mean in his wish for Paris to be humiliated, or is his a cry for his country's independence? What if Julian had maintained his loyalty to the Christian king instead of betraying him out of loyalty to his daughter and her honour? What if Badawi al-Jabal had understood better the truth of fascism and had chosen to forget his country's humiliation for the sake of democracy?

The question does not belong to some remote past. We could lure ourselves into believing that, in our epoch that imagines itself as 'without camps or blocs, without enemies and friends, the duel between heroes and imposters, between the good guys and the bad guys has gone, and has given way to the End of History and to democratic melancholy. Our epoch has widened the scope of the values it is prepared to recognize; it has made things more confused and complicated; it has not abandoned its heroes, but now reckons with counter-heroes as well. Politics is still a terrain of confrontation between multiple values and interests, and when things are not going well in our modern societies, the old mechanisms of sanctifying and demonizing creep back in triumph, as in the good old archaic days. For until now we have been incapable of 'thinking of Cain without Abel, or of Marcus Antonius without Augustus'. If best-selling biographers are doing well with the demolition of our favourite heroes – see the recent assaults on figures such as Bertold Brecht, Bruno Bethelheim, Graham Greene and Walt Disney – it is because we still have a psychic need to invest in illustrious figures of history.

Whereas heroes enjoy the taste of death, which holds no terrors in the face of their immutable faith in the cause they serve, the reverse is not true for traitors or cowards. Traitors are not always seekers of life, nor are they always motivated by greed and cowardice. They face our judgement with more complicated challenges. Heroes may or may not impress us. We may glorify their image or ignore them. But we cannot ignore traitors and cowards. The humiliation that they release in their passing – be it inflicted on them or by them – is far more disturbing and ambivalent than matters of pride and glory.

During the Nazi occupation the French sent more than three million anonymous letters in which they denounced their fellow citizens to the occupying authorities and the collaborationist government. As Cocteau wrote angrily, 'there are anonymous letters that are signed.' One of these signed letters was written by a man informing the police about a Jewish family hiding in a place that he could direct them to. In the same letter the man asks if the police could return his favour by letting him have the Jewish lady's fur coat to give to his wife. When we reach numbers like this, we are not looking at exceptional behaviour. Such debased behaviour is not specific to France, nor to the period either. Such numbers speak of rather ordinary behaviour, the behaviour of ordinary men and women and not of monsters. 'Monsters exist, but there are very few of them to present any real danger. Those who are dangerous are the ordinary men,' says Primo Levi. And precisely because they are ordinary they concern us more, and challenge our sense of sureness about ourselves and our fellow humans.

Traitors and cowards upset us and disturb our easy classification of things. I always think that the appeal of the film *Casablanca* is due not just to the charm of Ingrid Bergman or the sexiness of a Bogart turned cynical because of hardened circumstances. Our attraction to it is not based merely on the suspense within the love triangle and the dilemma of passion and duty; it owes a lot to the character of the sleazy police prefect played by Claude Rains. He incarnates *par excellence* the personality of a traitor, an unprincipled coward and an informer. His stature is not very imposing, being shorter than the other characters, his eyes are small, and his answers shifty. He shows deference to the powerful – a German officer in this case – and arrogant superiority in his lack of compassion for the weak – the penniless refugees stuck in Casablanca. Director Michael Curtiz wanted an entertaining movie and probably one that was not anti-French. His 'collaborator' is not an entirely detestable figure; in fact Capitaine Louis is actually somehow likeable. He is the ordinary, the unheroic, personified, and is not the other face of the coin to the Resistance fighters. He is very, very ordinary.

Why don't we hate him? Is it because we sense that the corrupt characters are less dangerous than the fanatics? Is it because we now know that totalitarian societies breed, and live off, very ordinary traitors and informers? And that people are left to choose between being mean or being impossible heroes? Treachery and betrayal are a necessary corollary to tyrannical authority and the violence of war.

Traitors pre-suppose a climate of war, and informers a climate of fear. They are partners to tyranny and grow within the social context that encourages them. Julian's reasons for betraying his Christian king were justified in his eyes by a higher set of values. In our own century it has been often in the name of some ideology that such tyranny has been exerted, creating heroes false and real, and traitors and informers of all kinds. Let us leave aside the Nazi ideology – Nazism excluded millions from showing courage or cowardliness, generosity or greed, and did not even give them the chance to be honest or opportunistic, and in this Nazism was outside humanity.

But what about other ideologies? Even some that claim to follow the road of liberalism. What about the Stalinist purges and the MacCarthyite witch-hunts? Both were products of societies that taught their youth that there was a time, an abhorrent time, when Christian faith had forgotten about toleration and those times were to be seen as the dark ages. Those times turned the defenders of faith into torturers for an absolute truth. Those old times were full of persecutors of the freedoms that people took with their souls and their beliefs. These were the times when Moslems could take pride in themselves for being more civilized and tolerant than the Catholic West, which was ruled by a church that turned its members into torturers, informants and bodies burning on crosses. Against memories of this kind the New World could hold up its liberal system of politics, while the communist regime sought to create a New Man.

It took a few centuries for this memory to fade before the needs of the rulers and their supporters asserted themselves. Then, both in the Soviet Union and in the United States, witch-hunting became acceptable again. The faith that lay behind this witch-hunt was not religion, but something similar – an exacerbated nationalism, or the purity of one's fidelity to the ideology of the system in place. And it went hand in hand with an obsession with security, meaning that any thinking that did not fit absolutely with the dominant thought was to be eradicated. In Russia, this purification killed millions. In the United States, it meant the loss of jobs and dignity for only a few hundreds. The difference is enormous and essential, but the spirit behind these purges is a reminder that we are not immune to the re-emergence of times when heroes and traitors proliferate.

Behind both purges lies not only a pursuit of ideological righteousness but also an obsession with traitors. In the Soviet Union, the belief in this truth meant that many ex-heroes of the revolution ended up admitting to being traitors to their nation. People who had resisted the oppression and the tortures of the Tsarist regime found their will broken when the system they fought for and believed in demonized them, and they ended up admitting to absurd crimes or accusing their colleagues of having betrayed the communist cause. The famous case of Pavlik Morozov, the 14-year-old child who denounced his father to the Stalinist authorities speaks for those terrible days. Pavlik declared that his father, who was a president of a *kolkhoz*, had helped the *Kulaks* to evade the state authorities. He was turned into a national hero, a myth of fidelity to communist values. He was seen as a great hero, because he had done what Gorki recommended: encouraging pioneers in the new generations to ignore parenthood based on blood relations and make them discover parenthood through the spirit. Gorki hoped that an 'engineering of the soul' might achieve this. The film-makers rose to a request to direct a film that would honour the boy's exploit. The film was never finished because the authorities found it too sophisticated for the cause of propaganda. Molozov himself was assassinated by members of the families of the kulaks whom his father, he claimed, had helped to escape. And there a fable of heroism and betrayal is brought to a most sinister end.

The United States during the 1950s was not a totalitarian society, or even a dictatorship, but it still fell into that dark gulf which societies fall into at some point in their history, when unhealthy passions take hold and the primitive instinct of annihilating the 'Other' turns into a crusade. These societies act as if they are at war, even when actual war is not in prospect. In the USA too informers were turned into heroes; and people who believed in loyalty and solidarity and did not want to harm their friends ended up being excluded. Here too people – mainly intellectuals and artists in this instance – reacted according to their nature and their beliefs to a situation that they could not control. Some with more or less courage, others with more or less cowardice.

Elia Kazan chose to cooperate with the un-American Activities Committee. He admitted past membership of the Communist Party, and named names. On 12 April 1952 he explained in the *New York Times* why he had done so: far from being an informer, he wrote, his action had been that of a man fighting for democracy. He declared that liberals ought to speak out, because secrecy was only beneficial to the communists, who had systematically raped the daily practices of democracy to which he adhered, and into which he had been trained.

A year or so later, Albert Einstein, also in the name of democracy, printed a desperate call to the intellectuals in the same newspaper asking them to refuse to cooperate, in the spirit of Ghandian resistance. Intellectuals, he said, should be ready to go to jail, to be ruined financially and to sacrifice their personal well-being for the cultural well-being of their country.

What Kazan forgot to mention was that what was going on

in the US was similar in its methods to what totalitarian regimes do all the time – divide their people into angels and devils, and create heroes, traitors, collaborators and victims. All in the name of some higher truth – a truth that is religious in nature even if it claims to be secular. Our modern societies may not care much about Florinda's virginity or the Cid's dilemmas between his love for Ximena and the duty he had to avenge his father's honour. But it still faces dilemmas in which other things are at stake – things that bring back the language of accusation and the terminology of praise. A language that is far from dead.

Symbols with Shaven Heads

Without you, Mrs Nomy, we might never have learnt at such an early age about the French resistance to the German occupation. You told us about the struggles and sacrifices of those who had fought the terror and the cruelty. You told us many stories about the fate of the victims. You read many poems that I was to return to later, searching for soothing words in the days of despair when war was killing on our own streets. What you did not tell your students, however, was how some of the victims reacted. Let me tell you a human tale narrated in black and white. Bear with me, for it is a long story. Revealed by a photographer who created it in a fraction of a second.

A few months ago I attended an exhibition of Magnum photographers. I came across Robert Capa's haunting photograph depicting the *tondue* (shaved woman) of Chartres. For me it was a reminder that the sad game of victims and victimizers is as old as history itself. When you look at the picture you know instantly who is the focus. She is in the middle. She is as centred as the image of Christ on the cross in depictions of the crucifixion. However, despite the centrality of the *tondue*, the image is not univocal. Its message is more complicated, more ambiguous than that of the crucifixion scene with Christ in the middle and a thief on either side. In fact all the characters are central. They each have a role to play. The victim is to be found everywhere, in each one of them, and there is a constant question mark over who exactly are the victimizers.

A picture shot in a fragment of a second tells a dramatic story of heroism and cowardice, of pardon and revenge, at a moment in European history. The struggle for survival in the midst of cruelty, and the cruelty inherited and internalized by the survivors themselves. A picture in black and white, catching its subjects just after the world had been divided by World War II. Looking at Capa's pictures, I know now why black and white pictures are more effective: in wars and revolutions there is no place for nuance. The line separating life from death, cruelty from compassion and friend from enemy is either horrifically black or unbearably white.

Her name is not to be told. This is as far as compassion goes. Her shaved head tells us all we need know about her. Her shaved head is there to be exhibited, like the hanging bodies at public executions. This woman, though, is not to be killed. She is to be humiliated. Her function in this performance is to exorcize the frustrations of the war's starved and exhausted survivors.

She is holding her baby. With a direct gaze she looks at the new life she brought into the world during the war. The father was possibly German. We can't tell if it is a look of love, that of an ordinary mother, or whether she is directing her gaze at the only place where she will not meet judgmental faces. Or maybe she is doing what they want her to do – looking at the baby as testimony of her treachery. Wherever we look at the other players in this performance, our eye always returns to the *tondue*, to her shaven head. She is the focus of all eyes, with one exception – the old man at the front of the picture. He is carrying somebody's belongings in a large bag. Whose? There is a puzzled expression on his face. He is the only one apart from the *tondue* and her baby who is not expressing enjoyment or curiosity. He looks slightly ashamed. Perhaps that is the way that we should all feel as we look at this dreadful, farcical spectacle.

The setting is carnivalesque. Most of the actors are enjoying the festival. Women, mostly undernourished and poorly dressed, are enjoying another woman's humiliation. The form of the humiliation is not bloody. Rather it is consciously directed against what is seen socially as the essence of femininity – the woman's hair. Or her lack of it. Children are brought along, either because the mothers didn't want to leave them alone at home or, more likely, so that they too can enjoy the show. The same happens when there is a carnival in town. The same happens in countries that carry out executions by hanging on Sundays. Fathers bring their children early, very early, in order to get a good place and the best view of the kicked-away chair and the distorted, agonized body.

In this snapshot fresco Robert Capa tells the story of all the *tondues*. He also tells us the story of all the others – all of us – when during a moment of ugliness we choose to share in the strength of the winner, and bury our own shame, doubts and anxieties in the savage ritual of punishment and the taking of revenge.

Who is this *tondue*? Some remnant of human decency has worked to erase her name and the names of all other *tondues* like her. Somebody would have pointed a finger at her at the moment when Chartres was liberated in August 1944. 'Look', they would have said, 'she is not skinny like us. She went to bed with a German. We suffered, we resisted, we were honourable French citizens, and we want to show it by seeing others being dishonoured. We had to lie low during the Occupation, and we grieved in silence, but now we want to yell and shout our lungs out. We have been insulted by the occupier, now we want to insult somebody ourselves. We are not heartless ... Look at this picture ... the atmosphere is that of a village feast ... Look how many of us are laughing and smiling. We're not burning witches here, we're just playing at it. The *tondue* will not be hurt physically, because we are not torturers. She will just be shamed. And our children who have been brought to watch will see that we are proud and upstanding. They will finally have a different image of us from all those years when we kept our heads lowered and our voices hushed.'

Capa narrows the angle at the back of the image, upsetting the laws of architectural perspective. The French flag stands guard over the crowd at the other end of the picture. This whole bizarre procession is in honour of that flag. The ritual is thus based on symbols. Symbols help to exorcize feelings. Here the age-old game of betrayal, shame, revenge and false heroism unfolds between the flag and the *tondue*. Between collaboration and victory, between fear and cowardice. Where is the true *Resistant*? I see no faces that speak of conviction in this picture. Perhaps the Resistance fighters did not need such mean evidence of their victory over Nazism. And where are the pretty French women we saw in the photos of civilians fleeing the bombs? Even then they had found time to dress well, to put on their high heels and their elegant hats. But in this carnival, this witch hunt, this pitiful charade of justice, the women have not bothered about their looks. Instead of high heels and nylon stockings they wear aprons over their dresses, and sandals and socks. You dress nicely when you are running for your life. You don't bother to look presentable and pretty when you celebrate a ritual of ugliness. You want to exhibit your misery, not run away from it.

The French collaboration with the Nazis was a dreadful story. But the victory celebrations were not always virtuous either. Where Hitler's genocide was engineered according to the most modern methods and techniques of the industrial age, the parades of the victors often appeared more inspired by the Middle Ages. All the shame, all the suffering inflicted by the Occupation, the frustration that people had to endure, were to be exorcized in this procession, where the sexual and the political were conflated to form the horrible image of the 'sexual collaborator'. A witch, a traitor, a threatening female.

Recently, during the celebrations surrounding the fiftieth anniversary of the Normandy landings, many spectres were unearthed. Questions about the collaboration of the French, the responsibility of the Germans and the 'heroism' of the Allied forces assailed us from all sides. I am sure, Mrs Nomy, that you were as hooked on the TV set as I was, and as addicted as I was to all the newspaper articles that looked back at the history of World War II. Suddenly we were transported back into what we had come to think of as a fading world of black and white. Questions like 'How dare the French, who were the first collaborators, refuse to allow the Germans to participate in the celebration of the victory over the Nazis?' were asked by a few journalists. Or with more assurance, phrases such as 'The Germans have not yet paid for their crimes' were uttered in the course of the martial celebration in the mass media. Fifty years later, people were still not immune to generalizing vocabularies. If we believe that lack of nuance is the hallmark of times of turmoil, wars and revolutions, and that a world in the midst of upheavals needs easy explanations for things, in which 'History is written in capital letters', then we need only look at photographic documents that are in black and white in order to begin to understand how all this could have happened.

Capa turns his camera into an eye that scrutinizes the human predicament. For Capa knew, as John Steinbeck put it so lucidly, that 'one cannot photograph war, for war is mainly emotion.' So Capa photographed the effects of war. His camera searched for images of betrayal and cowardice as much as of heroism and generosity. What constitutes his photos are the same ingredients that determined our human history. We carry these ingredients with us just as we carry our own bodies in which both agility and awkwardness combine. When we punish traitors we are fighting the temptation of the traitor within us. When we worship heroes, we are wanting the excellence that is in them to arise from where it lies within us too.

The *tondue* is an easy target for the exorcism of our fears and frustrations. All the more so because she is female and

entangled in the most uncontrollable issues of human life –
death and sexual desire. Her persecution is that of a 'criminal',
who is also a victim, by a crowd of the righteous. Their self-
assurance is bolstered by their numbers in a mechanism as
old as time itself. Adulterous women were – and in some parts
of the world still are – punished in the same manner, and here
the method is used on women who are judged to have
committed adultery against the whole nation. In the
photograph fear has evaporated with the defeat of Germany,
so the masses can afford the joyful carnival atmosphere that
Capa has caught with his camera. Capa's photography tells us
shrewdly, and in an austere and dignified way, about the effect
of war and its humiliations. He speaks through the expressions
on the faces of his subjects. He speaks by making us see faces
that are distressing to look at.

Capa uses his camera in the same way that Zola used words.
When I read *Germinal* as a teenager, I felt the violence of war
(Zola's class war), and frustration, before I actually understood
the concepts behind the book. For weeks I would wake in the
middle of the night with images of the women tearing the
shopkeeper to pieces. The shopkeeper symbolized the root of
the miners' starvation. He had to be dehumanized physically,
by dehumanized masses, and forced to eat wood, in order to
assuage their demonizing hunger.

Later when I became part of the Left movement I always
felt somehow uneasy among the crowds at demonstrations. I
would fight my fear, my *Germinal* memories, by screaming the
slogans all the louder. Like all real artists, Zola had influenced
me in contradictory ways. I was going to revolt against injustice

and exploitation, but I would fear the victims' eventual metamorphosis. Victims all too easily conditioned to become victimizers. To make his point, Zola had chosen the weakest, oldest woman and had her doing something dreadful – holding up the shopkeeper's amputated sex and raising it high like a trophy. Fortunately in Capa's photograph there is no blood. The attack on the sexuality of the woman traitor is symbolic. It is her hair, the symbol of her femininity, that will fall before the eyes of the crowd.

The famous French singer Arletty, to whom it is said we owe the everlasting *rouge baiser* lipstick (she had to find a lipstick that would survive the multitude of kisses she distributed during her show, many of which went to the German officers who were being entertained in occupied Paris) was too powerful to be *tondue*. On hearing of the fate meted out to women accused of 'sexual collaboration' she declared ironically: '*Quoi! On veut se mêler de nos affaires de cul maintenant?*' ('What! They want to interfere in the business of our cunts now?')

Eluard's anger at the fate of the *tondues* came out in the form of a moving poem. A poem that was influential, given that it came from a communist at a time when the communists were in a winning position. In condemning the acts of revenge perpetrated against those poor women, he lamented the fate of womanhood as a whole – the fate of beauty, as he put it, perhaps a touch awkwardly, in that pre-feminist age:

Comprenne qui voudra
Moi mon remords ce fut

La malheureuse qui resta
Sur le pavé
La victime raisonable
A la robe dechirée
Au regard d'enfant perdue
Decouronnée defigurée
Celle qui ressemble aux morts
Qui sont morts pour être aimés

Une fille faite pour un bouquet
Et couverte du noir crachat des tenèbres

Une fille galante
Comme une aurore de premier mai
La plus aimable bête

Souillée et qui n'a pas compris
Qu'elle est souillée
Une bête prise au piège
Des amateurs de beauté

Et ma mère la femme
voudrait bien dorloter
cette image idéale
de son malheur sur terre

(Paul Eluard, *Au rendez-vous allemand*, 1944)

The power of Eluard's poem lies not only in his contrasting of ugliness and beauty and his counterposing of innocence and freshness to shame and obscenity. It is in his portrayal of this morbid, farcical concentration on the plight of womanhood. The fate of this *tondue* is the fate of his mother – his very own mother – who herself suffers for being a woman.

The problem with Eluard is that he leaves us with questions: What if the woman was not that innocent? What if she was not a symbol of the eternal feminine, the sweet beauty of desired passive femininity? What if she did not just love a German soldier, but also served the German occupiers in exchange for favours? After all, many novels, films and works of art in the period after the Second World War did sing the praises of love over and against national or group allegiance. Edith Piaf, for instance, gave us goose pimples each time she sang passionately: *J'irais jusqu'au bout du monde, je me ferais teindre en blonde, je renierais ma patrie, je renierais mes amis, si tu me le demandais.* What then? Would our compassion for this woman fade away? Would we find ourselves again facing the dilemmas of judgment, understanding, forgetting, and seeking a preventive justice?

There is no easily available road to simple justice, as Camus regretted in 1945. He deplored the term *épuration* that was current in France in that period. He referred to it as 'The thing that became horrid. It had a small chance of not becoming so, which meant that it had to be conceived in a spirit free of revenge or lightness. One has to believe that the road to a simple justice is not easy to find between the shouting for hatred on one hand and the claims of bad consciences on the other. Justice is not always the opposite of terror.'

I have continued the story that you began, Mrs Nomy, but the stories of victims and victimizers interweave in curious ways. Their memory is woven like Penelope's tapestry.

Homelands

Many years have passed since the day when she hung up on Abu Firas. She now lives on her own. Allen and she are separated. He could no longer stand the hurried pace of the city. She feels at home in London, more than he ever did. Now she is a British national, but sees herself more as a citizen of Kensington. This is her real and true nation. When people come to visit from Lebanon or France, she is proud to walk them through the park, along the path by the Serpentine, and she always pauses at the same spot on the bridge so that they can admire the reflections of the trees in the placid surface of the water. Then she walks them up Kensington Church Street and tells them about the obsessive passion of the English for the past and its antiquities, their weakness for mahogany chests and the imposing bronze frames that glitter through the classy shop windows along the ascending road. She would always end her tour in a part of London that had no concern for periods, be they past or future: Portobello Road. There, amid a feast of juxtaposed sounds and cultures, she would ask her visitors if they had ever witnessed such an exciting mixture of styles and customs in their own countries. She now feels alien in cities that are not confused in their identities, cities with linear and local memories. She needs hybridity and clashes of colours in order to fit.

Why did she suddenly decide to go back to Beirut? She was happy as a Londoner and felt no need for big changes in her life. Smooth was the word that best described the routine of her existence here. She even resented those rare occasions when she had to visit the northern or eastern parts of the city. So why did she suddenly feel like being back in Lebanon? Was it perhaps because of the insistent presence of a pile of letters that she had written to Mrs Nomy without ever having tried to find a forwarding address for her? They had actually turned into a book, a book that would probably never be sent to a publisher either. Whatever the reason, she decided that looking back was necessary and somehow the only thing to do now.

Her first step was to trace the whereabouts of Abu Firas. He had never tried to contact her again after that phone call that had triggered her suppressed recollections and so troubled her mind. His people had been moved to new countries, new refuges, and then on once again to other places. Now that she had a safe home, now that she was firmly settled among other exiles in a cosy homeland of blissful and stable marginality, she felt that she owed it to him, the wanderer who had never been given a chance to settle and choose.

'You didn't know?' the old woman said, in an unresolved voice that hesitated between outrage and weariness. 'He died when that wretched bomb blew half of this neighbourhood away. Many people died that day. They showed it on TV all over the world. Where were you then, on Mars?' It obviously meant a lot to her that the explosion of the bombs and their ravages didn't go unnoticed in the outside world. Living and suffering in a ghetto is bad enough, but the thought of it having been forgotten is unbearable.

She didn't answer. What good would a truthful answer do for this poor old woman? No, the TV channels were bored with the endless bombings. They weren't news any longer, and they weren't good for viewer ratings either. Even the most nostalgic of Lebanese exiles stopped zapping like mad addicts for the latest news update from Lebanon after a few years in exile. The wrinkled features of the old woman begged for reassurance. She needed to hear that there were still people out there who remembered them and cared about their misery; that her family was not going to rot, silently forgotten, in these muddy slums; that there were people outside who still cared. The old woman smiled, and in an obvious effort to be cheerful said: 'It is all written. It is destiny. Did you hear about the man who escaped unharmed from an explosion that killed all the other people who were in the building with him? He decided to emigrate to Canada. Only one week after he landed there, he fell on the stairs of a restaurant, and died instantly from a brain haemorrhage. When your time has come, there is nothing you can do, no precautions you can take.' Such stories abounded in Lebanon. They carried a therapeutic power that no person living in safety and security could ever understand. Rationality is the privilege of the safe and the happy.

She did not dare ask if this bomb was actually intended to kill *him*. These bombs never made any sense. They were aimed at streets and buildings and anyone who happened to be in them. Nor did it make sense trying to find out who had been behind it. There was a time when these mass killings were such an everyday reality that you could as well have accused a jealous husband. So he died. He faded away. Like Umm Ali. Like Hashem. Like so many people who never had the chance to end up in Kensington, or the *XVIème arrondissement*, or even, for that matter, the slums of Detroit.

She walked out of the camp, shattered. She found she was missing the busy, cluttered streets of Sabra. She was missing their narrowness, and the kids playing in them, and the voices of the mothers calling their children back in. Now the camp is like an abandoned island in the middle of Beirut. There are only old people on the doorsteps, and a few idle adolescents. The camp is dry and screams from the lack of running water. The Lebanese want to forget their wars. They decided to forget the refugees who had been left behind, who had not been driven away to new refuges. These are the victims of amnesia, except that they are to be forgotten but not forgiven. The camp looks like one of those Dali paintings in which time hangs from a floppy watch, stagnating and lost among vestiges of lives and monstrous nightmares. Beirut is growing and putting up new and optimistic buildings. In an incitement to bitterness, those buildings are clearly visible from the old woman's shack.

The old woman was smoking a locally-made cigarette and staring into nowhere. She thanked the old woman for her invitation to come inside and drink tea with her. She knew that the old woman needed her solitude as much as she did at that moment. She walked out of the camp as if she was moving across time. Time was terribly still and stagnant in there. But just a few metres away, the insistent noise of pneumatic drills was speaking of a fast, impatient leap into the future. Here buildings were mushrooming as if emulating the animated images of some cartoon film. Reality was becoming a parody of art, and her old city was like a difficult puzzle, with contrasting and conflicting pieces waiting for some magical hand to fit them back together. She stood at the opposite corner of the roundabout, at the outer edge of the camp. There was no physical wall, no actual barbed wire separating the camp from the rest of the city. But they were there none the less. She saw them in the eyes of the old woman, and in the rapid, hurried glances of the passers-by at the roundabout.

She stood there waiting for a taxi. She was agitated and angry at herself for not having inquired about Abu Firas earlier. Could it be that the relentless pounding of the drills had got to her brain and thrown her off balance? Somebody should tell them to turn off the power for a moment, just to allow the rest of us to listen to the silence of the camp. She screamed aloud as if needing to test the power of her own voice against the din of the machines. Maybe after all there should have been some trials, some assessment of responsibility in this terrible war. You can't wipe out ugly memories without also erasing some of your humanity.

She could no longer wait for the taxi. She started walking, ignoring the dusty, raucous promise of the future, with its drills. She was thinking of Mrs Nomy. She was ready to write a new essay for her. She needed to write. She needed to forget the bitter taste of the air on that roundabout. She longed for some of the past to get off her chest and settle into words.

Responsibility, Truth and Punishment

An Essay for Mrs Nomy

I am responsible for killing 30 people with my own hands ... But I would be a hypocrite if I said that I am repentant for what I did. I don't repent, because I am convinced that I was acting under orders, and that we were fighting a war ... We were killing human beings, but still we continued ... I have spent many nights sleeping in the *plazas* of Buenos Aires with a bottle of wine, trying to forget.

These are the words of Adolfo Francisco Scilingo, a 48-year-old retired Argentinian naval commander. If I had heard his name in another context, I might have imagined a charming man with a tan, an exquisite smile, and the relaxed elegance of a tango dancer. But then who ever said that being a tango dancer was in contradiction to being an executioner? Scilingo was one of the protagonists in the 'Dirty War' of the 1970s which left Argentina traumatized and has created an organization of mothers searching for clues about their disappeared sons and daughters.

Mr Scilingo was one of those who had something to do with the disappearances, and Mr Scilingo decided to speak.

To speak, but not to repent. He chose to speak out because of what he called the Navy's indifference to the plight of the rank and file who had carried out the orders for the torturing and killing of prisoners.

Adolfo Scilingo was a naval commander. He has his reasons for speaking. He feels he has been treated unjustly by the post-dictatorship press. He says that he does not feel guilty, but that he still needs the bottle to help him forget. His words are sometimes arrogant, often pitiful, and at best contradictory.

He told his terrible story in 1995. More than sixteen years after the killings had ended. He told us how the Argentinian military dictatorship had disposed of up to two thousand prisoners – having first kidnapped and tortured them – by dumping them into the Atlantic Ocean.

Many of the victims were so weak from torture and detention that they had to be helped aboard the plane. Once in flight, they were injected with a sedative by an Argentine Navy doctor before two officers stripped them and shoved them to their deaths. [Calvin Sims, 'New Horrors from Argentina's "Dirty war"', *New York Herald Tribune*, 14 March 1995]

Fifty years earlier, Colonel (now General) Paul Tibbetts Jr had chosen the name that baptized an airplane that was about to set out on an historical mission. The *Enola Gay*. A tender gesture. Enola Gay was the name of the colonel's mother. The airplane, a B-29 Super Fortress, was under his command when it dropped the H-bomb on Hiroshima. When asked recently on Canadian TV whether he didn't sometimes feel remorse and whether he regretted having killed so many people, he answered without a hint of hesitation that it never stopped him from sleeping, and that he saw no reason why he should be ashamed. 'It was like that'.

I cannot help feeling anger with these two gentlemen. Somewhere inside me lurks a stupid desire to hear them voice regret. As if their regret could make me feel more secure. As if history were a simple matter that can be read in simple ways and diverted to new beginnings and bright new futures for all.

But let's think about General Tibbetts for a minute. It must have been nerve-wracking for him to find himself a hero at one moment, only to be turned into a monster mass killer the next, when the political mood in the United States changed. He is now, and has been for the last fifty years, a central character in a debate that has divided America. In one view he is a hero, in the other a villain with no compassion. Heroes and villains need each other and feed on each other, so it is not surprising to find them role-switching in the drama that real life stages for them. It is no concern of generals and officers to be assessing whether history is an exact science or not, still less to be asking moral questions. And what Hannah Arendt wanted to know was 'what made this man stop thinking?'. She was not speaking of a hero but a bureaucrat, a member of a party: Eichmann was not a soldier.

General Tibbetts has to live with his past, and at a certain level his reaction is understandable. What is not so understandable is when, fifty years later, an editorial writer in the *Washington Post* proclaims, in line with the known views of Bill Clinton, that America owes Japan no apology for the nuclear bombs that were used on Hiroshima and Nagasaki. Clinton had made a speech to the effect that President Harry Truman had made a correct choice, 'based on the facts he had before him'. The editorial writer feels that this justificatory sub-clause is not required. Why? Because, among other things, 'to put it mildly, Japan's imperial army was never distinguished by any great concern for the civilian populations unfortunate enough to come within its reach.'

I don't know why the columnist did not finish this last sentence with 'So why should we have been?' Or 'An eye for an eye and a tooth for a tooth'. Perhaps he feared that in expressing himself so frankly he might have been accused of barbarism! [*International Herald Tribune*, 18 April 1995]

I am interested in General Tibbetts and Mr Scilingo, because in the unpleasant business of calling for the truth to be known we have to call in all the principal actors. When these actors speak some unpleasant truth, we have to accept it as a reality that exists, a reality that may be the fruit of circumstances but is also the fruit of our human condition. The question keeps coming back to me: was Said evil, or was he evil because of the war? Might I have become like Said if I had lived in the same flat, had the same mother, and had the same frustrations when the war engulfed my street?

'We went to the airport, we entered through the back gate, we loaded the subversives in, like zombies, and we embarked them on the aeroplane.' These are the words of Scilingo describing the processes in which he was twice a participant. [*Courier International*, 16–22 March 1995]

When asked whether today he would still call the people who were thrown into the sea subversives, Scilingo says: 'No ... when I did what I did it was understood that they were subversive. Now I can't say that they were. They were human beings. We were so sure then that nobody asked questions ... It was not a small group [of military people who took part in these flights]. The entire marines were involved.'

When asked by his interviewer if this was not particularly cowardly behaviour, to throw people to their death in the ocean when they had been led to believe that they were being transferred to another jail, Scilingo answers: 'If you look at it that way, it is possible. It is not normal, now I know that.'

Scilingo insists that he was following orders. A handful of marines had refused to obey these orders. To Scilingo and his ilk, they were cowards. To us, and to the victims and their families and comrades, they come across as the real heroes. The times when one has no choice but to be either a hero or a traitor are not the most human of times. 'Woe betide nations that must have heroes,' says Brecht. Unfortunately, we cannot add 'Happy are the nations that must have cowards,' for there is no way that you can have the one without the other.

The temptation to forget, to turn the page and pass on is extremely strong. To finish once and for all with phrases like the 'Lessons of History'. In Europe I tried to change my skin, as we say in my native tongue. I went on for years rejecting politics. I thought I could keep my hands clean by keeping away from it. I proudly paid all the parking tickets that appeared on my windscreen and took this as a token that now I belonged to a stable, civilized society in which people should respect their duties and keep within the law. This proved rather heavy on my pocket, since I never lost my Beirut instinct to park wherever I found an empty space. I trawled the art galleries of Paris and London looking for an art that was not concerned with social issues. I praised fun, kitsch and lightness. The intention of my sculptures was that they should be colourful, superficial and useless. They were made to enjoy themselves, arrogantly, to indulge eternally in a trance of fun that no conflict could ever interrupt. I painted them in silver and gold, and I painted my own lips with a striking red. (Are you still wearing those austere brown suits, Mrs Nomy? Or have you too opted for extravagant colours, to defy the grey memories of our lands?) Long live escapism was the slogan by which I lived. But long it could not live. I find myself unable to switch off the TV when I see boys with faces like that of Said, but now speaking in Serbo-Croat. I search for clues in the confessions of Scilingo. I compare the twisted face of Leila's grandmother to the sweet wrinkles on the face of Nelson Mandela.

Mandela left his jail and threw his energies into the future, whereas you, Fadwa, dragged your life into the past. His humiliations and those of his people made him hate the act of humiliation; your humiliation, on the other hand, turned into a desire to humiliate, a desire that was fed by a relentless, insatiable, morbid energy. Remembering your bitterness, Fadwa, I cling to the example of Nelson Mandela, and I set great store by his decision to pardon and forgive and to turn the ugliest past into a bright new future. The defenders of apartheid will be pardoned for crimes, or so Mandela promised shortly after his election as president of South Africa. And he promised that there would be no dismantling of the symbols and monuments that were dear to the whites, not without intense, patient, serious discussion.

'Most white police officers and others who killed or tortured in defence of apartheid would be given indemnity for their crimes and would not be publicly named.' [*International Herald Tribune*, 2 May 1994] The government of Nelson Mandela created a Commission for Truth and Reconciliation that had a mandate to create 'understanding but not vengeance' for the past, 'reparation but not retaliation'.

Here the victims are not acting as victims. They are acting as the best of human beings. You, Fadwa, only succeeded in making your husband's old age miserable and your own life impermeable to fun and tenderness. You were as solid as a rock, for resentment has the texture of heavy metal while forgiving is conceived by a melting of substance. That is why I am afraid when I think of Mandela, and that is why I keep my fingers crossed when I look to South Africa.

Some South Africans say that forgiving and forgetting would be a recipe for disaster. They say that a full amnesty would not help reconciliation, that a failure to deal with the gross abuses of apartheid would only leave the wounds of the past festering. Understanding unacceptable behaviour encourages unacceptable behaviour – so says the futurist Robert Theobald, in another context. But is there one position that we can say is a correct position? This question keeps coming back to us as we confront the endless list of situations in which atrocities are the norm. From the horrors of the Holocaust to the appalling scenes in Rwanda, from the starving prisoners in Serbian concentration camps to the blood-filled stadium where Pinochet kept his prisoners in Chile, and then to the indiscriminate massacres by Moslems and Christians alike in my own country – to all this our answers and solutions never seem to be adequate. And they are certainly never sufficiently preventive. Should harsh punishment – as one might conclude from the futurist's statement – be the answer? Should we believe that the South African model will succeed, and should we take the example of Chile, where Pinochet and his friends now live a perfectly normal life? Might we agree with President Menem of Argentina that the people who are spreading scandals and promoting Scilingo's revelations are muckrakers who care nothing for the reconstruction of the country?

It is as tempting to believe in the merits of amnesia as it is to jump to the sad and pessimistic conclusion that what happened to you in the past inevitably determines how you will behave in the future. Howard Jacobson expressed in poignant terms the inevitable ugliness of the victims' response, in a newspaper article on Baruch Goldstein's bloody attack on the Palestinians who were praying in the Hebron Mosque, in which dozens of Arabs were killed in a hail of machine-gun fire. He called his article 'What Baruch did to God': 'Out of martyrology grows demonology. Put it how you like: worms turn, ugly ducklings become swans, victims acquire a taste for perpetration, cowards decide it's time to be heroes.' [*The Independent*, 5 March 1994]

Latifa did not turn into an ugly worm. But who today any longer remembers what she – or Umm Ali – looked like? Her victimizers were happy to see her vanish, and her former comrades had plenty of other martyrs to boast of and had no need to be dealing with her. She was a useless hero who hadn't been smart enough to leave behind a photograph for her future glorification into martyrdom and further acts of revenge.

Truth. You were pretty strict on this subject, Mrs Nomy. In fact, I would say that you were actually a bit rigid. There was another time when I incurred your disapproval for my writing. You had given us a very simple title for a French-language essay. The old chestnut: 'Describe in three pages how you spent your weekend'. It never occurred to me that my account was expected to be realistic, so I proceeded to describe the scene in 'our country cottage'. I wrote about how my father sat peacefully and solemnly in his imposing armchair next to the fireplace, smoking his ebony pipe. I told of the leather-bound book that I placed on his lap, and the sheepdog that sat at his feet. I showed my mother gardening and myself playing on the grass. You thoroughly disapproved of this imagined weekend. You called it a lie: 'This comes directly from some French novel that you must have been reading,' you said. 'It has nothing to do with the truth of your own reality. I wish you had been truthful. Good writing is when writing is sincere. *Truth* is what I expect from a good student.'

Perhaps, Mrs Nomy, your aim was to teach us not to be culturally imperialized. But I cannot agree with your definition of writing. In a creative work one can be sincere and untruthful at the same time. Maybe it was true, perhaps I had read too many books by the Comtesse de Ségur and maybe my imagination had placed me in the cottage of one of her (and my) heroines. Literature has always been obsessed with the puzzle of truth. Tragedy pounds endlessly on with dilemmas of revenge and punishment, love and forgiveness. Tragedy still entertains us with the dilemmas that politics can't be bothered with.

In the early 1990s, a modern tragedy, Ariel Dorfman's *Death and the Maiden*, rose to sudden world acclaim [Nick Hern Books, London, 1992]. It was written at a time when the question of amnesty for torturers was being raised in many parts of the world. It was censored in Chile, its country of origin. It was performed for the first time at the ICA in London in 1990. (This was thanks to a woman who died too young – Linda Brandon, an intelligent and lively organizer of talks at the ICA.) Dorfman had written a play about three characters caught in a triangle of torture, revenge and retribution.

Let me tell you about it. I have no idea where you are living now, and whether you will ever see it, but discussing it will help me begin the debate that I never had with you, about truth as an absolute virtue.

Gerardo Escobar is the husband of Paulina Salas. He sits on the commission that has been set up to investigate the crimes of the Chilean dictatorship. He is a lawyer, and he supported the commission's decision that it would neither name nor judge the perpetrators of these crimes. One day, on his way home, Gerardo has a problem with his car, and a pleasant-mannered man, Dr Roberto Miranda, sees him in trouble and helps him out. Gerardo invites this pleasant Dr Miranda back to his house as a way of thanking him for his help. Paulina is distressed when she sees the visitor. She is sure that he is the doctor who supervised her torture. She wants him punished. When her husband questions her need for revenge, Paulina sequesters Dr Miranda, ties him up, and threatens to kill him unless he confesses. When Gerardo tries to reason with her, his arguments are those of a politician, or a person who believes in forgiveness in order to rebuild. He begs his wife to set the doctor free:

'Yes. If he's guilty, more reason to let him go. Don't look at me like that. You want to scare these people and provoke them, Paulina, till they come back, make them so insecure that they come back to make sure we don't harm them . . . You satisfy your own personal passion, you punish on your own, while the other people in this country with scores of other problems who finally have a chance to solve some of them, those people can go screw themselves – the whole transition to democracy can go screw itself.'

Paulina – like the heroine of a revenge tragedy – feels betrayed. She keeps asking, 'What about me?' She expressed her burning need for justice. 'You know what I was thinking of? Doing to them, systematically, minute by minute, instrument by instrument, what they did to me . . . I was horrified at myself. That I should have such hatred in me, that I should want to do something like that to a defenceless human being, no matter how vile.'

Revenge tragedies are built around the notion of a person prosecuting a crime in a private capacity, a sort of sublime vigilante. Unlike the figure played by Charles Bronson in the popular movies, they are deeply torn about the only solutions that seem open to them. Heroes of revenge tragedies have to take matters into their own hands because society has failed to establish justice through its normal channels. Paulina is the perfect heroine of a terrible affliction. She is denied even the satisfaction of the recognition of their misdeeds by her torturers and rapists, let alone seeing them punished.

I don't know Dorfman's own personal stance on these questions. His strength is that we are alternately convinced by the mutually contradictory arguments of both Paulina and her husband. How can we choose to hide the truth, forget, and hope for a better future, he seems to be asking. At the same time he puts into Gerardo's mouth words that transcend the political narrowness of the situation and invites us, to join Gerardo in begging Paulina to forgive. For her own sake, even, we like Gerardo, want her to forget. 'Look at you love,' he tells her tenderly. 'You're still a prisoner, locked up with them [her torturers] in that basement ...'

Sometimes Dorfman joins Jacobson in his suggestion that the victimizer engulfs the victim into his frame of mind – 'victims acquire a taste for perpetration'. At other times he joins those who prefer to forgive and think only of the future – of healing instead of the search for justice. For instance, in his afterword to the play he asks:'How do we forget without risking its [the atrocities implemented by the dictatorship] repetition in the future? Is it legitimate to sacrifice the truth to ensure peace?'

Is Paulina pushing us to 'blame the victim'? 'Imagine what

would happen if everyone acted like you did. You satisfy your own personal passion, you punish on your own.'

∼∾∽

After having seen some awful reactions from the 'victims' in Lebanon's Civil War, I have more problems than I used to with justifications of and allowances for the victim's reactions. I can understand a victim needing to regain his or her self-esteem. I can understand them calling for retribution. But the savagery inflicted by the Holocaust is no justification for the humiliations imposed by the Israeli State on the Palestinians. Many Jews reacted with the utmost humanity after what they had been through. Many came out saying: 'Never again should we allow this to happen to any human being.' Their victimization had turned them not into perpetrators, but into devoted partisans of a better world, a world that abhors torture, racism, and national discrimination. Most Holocaust victims did not turn into perpetrators. And if a few did, ex-victims or not, they are to be blamed. Rarely does a woman who has been raped wish to see her aggressor raped. Equally rare are the women who would take a hammer to destroy the person they see as responsible for the death of a brother. When I saw this happen, I knew it was a terrible exception.

Primo Levi, in *The Truce*, tells a story that says more than any essay or study about humanity's dilemma when it faces the choice between pardon and revenge. In this book he tells of what happened to him and his fellow prisoners after the Red Army had freed them from Auschwitz, as they were trying to find their way back home. They wandered for several months in Central Europe, hungry and miserable, thanks to the bureaucratic blunders of the Russian administration. Levi and his fellow inmates ended up in Zhmerinka. All he could say about the place was that it was located some 300 km (190 miles) from the city of Odessa. By then he and his companions had been reduced to begging in order to survive. In Zhmerinka they had an encounter,

> which destiny had organized ... A dozen German prisoners, like unattended cattle ... as far as we could see, they had been forgotten, simply abandoned to their fate ... They saw us, and some of them waved towards us with the uncertain steps of automata. They asked for bread; not in their own language, but in Russian. We refused, because our bread was precious. But Daniele did not refuse; Daniele whose strong wife, whose brother, parents and no less than thirty relatives had been killed by the Germans; Daniele, who was the sole survivor of the raid on the Venice ghetto, and who from the day of the liberation had fed on grief, took out a piece of bread, showed it to these phantoms, and placed it on the ground. But he insisted that they come to get it dragging themselves on all fours, which they did docilely.

Levi does not elaborate on the story. He simply tells it. He provides evidence, as the indefatigable testifier. For testifying, in the view of Daniele Sallenave, is 'the ultimate relationship we can have with the dead; testifying is to be their voice, their messenger, their interpreter. The witness cannot discharge himself from the anguish and the fault of having survived; he can however charge himself with the mission of transmitting. The debt towards the dead is transformed into a duty towards those who are not yet born.' Primo Levi simply transmits this terrifying little story and leaves the difficult task of drawing conclusions to us. Daniele, the victim who had suffered most among this group of survivors, whom we might have expected to wish the death of the German soldiers, was the only one who gave them food. His generosity is almost unbearable. But he did not just give his bread; he gave a terrible lesson too. A lesson in the nature of humiliation. The soldiers had to be shown what it meant to have to accept dehumanization – to be reduced to the posture of animals – if they wanted to survive. Or was it that Daniele was taking a small revenge by telling them 'I am better than you ... I will help you survive, but first I will have my little revenge and enjoy seeing you humiliated, just as you humiliated me when I was helpless'?

One day the people of ex-Yugoslavia, like those of Lebanon before them, will be able to wake up without the sounds of bullets and go to sleep without needing to shelter from missiles. What will they do about those who killed their loved ones, raped their women, and tortured their prisoners? Would they say in time of peace Borislav Herak will become a 'normal' human being again? Like I hope Said had become even though I do not dare get close enough to find out. Herak was a nice (albeit failed) soldier in Yugoslavia before the war, his brother-in-law was a Bosnian Muslim, and they got along very well. But in the chaotic bloody rage of the war of hatred, he became not only a Bosnian hater, but also a male who would try to use his other weapon, his penis, in order to inflict a humiliation that the firing weapons could not inflict. Did Said rape any women?

Were all these terrible acts committed by people who had simply been '*pris dans un engrenage*'? – 'caught up in a machine' – the words used by François Mitterrand to justify the leniency shown to René Bousquet, the Vichy regime's police chief from April 1942 to December 1943. Bousquet was responsible for the arrest of 13,152 Jews, including 4,115 children.

> Bousquet was a high official who was *pris dans un engrenage* . . . Bousquet was a prototype of these high officials who were compromised or who allowed themselves to be compromised to a degree.

It would be too easy to explain Mitterrand's attitude by reference to his political past, and all the discussions about his own WWII career that featured in the press and on TV during his final days in power. His plea – 'We cannot live all the time on these memories and this rancour' – was that of a man who knew how it is possible for people to change, and who wanted to be remembered as the president who abolished capital punishment in France. Pompidou once said something similar, commenting many years earlier on France's recurring scandals and tales of heroism, a legacy from the years of Nazi occupation: 'I hate all that business', he said. 'I hate medals, I hate decorations of all kinds.'

Simone Veil, the French Gaullist and ex-minister, was herself a victim of the likes of Bousquet. She was deported during the Occupation. Her account of her reaction upon learning that she had been 'denounced as a Jew' lacked any sense of vengefulness. She did not try to find out who had given her away, who had betrayed her. To those who commented on her lack of curiosity she replied with beautiful simplicity:

Deep down, I was not interested. I would have been interested to know why and how people had been drawn into this climate of denunciation. Or why responsible politicians or administrators, as well as intellectuals, could be drawn in certain circumstances to accept certain things ... because the question could still be raised, even forty years later. [*Le Monde*, 23–4 January 1983]

One day the people of Iraq will be rid of the horrifying oppressor who has so distorted their lives. Saddam Hussein cannot survive for ever. One day they will be able to look forward to a freer life, and an end to the punishment that the International Community has inflicted on them (while signally failing to inflict it on their oppressor). What will happen if they decide to look backwards at the same time as looking forward?

Inspired by the Nuremberg trials, the Iraqi Opposition issued a report entitled *Crimes Against Humanity and the Transition from Dictatorship to Democracy* (a report commissioned by the Executive Council of the Iraqi National Congress, May 1993) which concludes:

The INC wants to follow that successful precedent [the amnesty announced by the Kurdish organizations on the eve of the Iraqi uprisings of March 1991, which brought over to the rebel side all the Kurdish auxiliary units in the Iraqi army] with a view to isolating those individuals responsible for leading, organizing, instigating or participating in the formulation or execution of grievous abuses of human rights in Iraq since 1979, the date of Saddam Hussein's ascension to the Presidency of the Republic . . . The all-encompassing amnesty referred to earlier covers all criminal acts against individual Iraqis committed by any army or civilian personnel up to June 1 1993, the official date of issuance of this report. It does not cover, however, any civil violations which might be legitimately brought against any Iraqi at a later date.

The concept of prescription for crimes committed before a certain date is obviously inspired by the restriction adopted at the Nuremberg trials. As for the reasoning behind the INC document, it is based on premises that are listed in the first chapter of the document:

There are crimes that are so serious as to mandate universal enforcement, jurisdiction, and responsibility. These are what the legal system calls *crimen contra omnes*, 'crimes against all'. Such crimes have been committed inside Iraq on a large scale since July 1979, following the accession of Saddam Hussein to the Presidency of the Republic in a bloody purge of the upper echelons of the Ba'th Command.

If such crimes are to be left unpunished, a terrible injustice will have been perpetrated upon the survivors of these crimes, along with their families. The suffering of the victims will not have been honored and redeemed by Iraqi society at large. This is bound to leave a legacy of bitterness and pain that will live on to haunt the Iraqi body politic for generations to come. The welfare of the victims, and of future generations of Iraqis, demands that justice be done and be seen to be done.

The document realizes the aberration that such a general statement might lead to. For in Iraq, much more extensively than in Chile or Argentina, and even more than in East Germany, something like a fifth of 'the economically active labor force in 1980 were institutionally charged with one form or another of violence (whether policing, defending, or controlling the society at large) . . . Many, if not most Iraqis, are simultaneously victims and victimizers.'

Obviously, nobody can try a fifth of a country's population, and without being very arbitrary it would be impossible to draw a line to define the degree of the crimes of this fifth part. Let alone the fact that the other four parts, due to the high ratio, are obviously brothers, sisters, spouses and parents of the members of that fifth part.

How to avoid a reaction like that of Paulina without at the same time falling into the hopeless cynicism of Mathias Wedel, the East German author of *Fellow Travellers*, a book in which he attacks fellow authors who wrote under the former Communist regime? When it became known that he himself had made reports to the Stasi, under the name of Milan (by now we realize that there was nothing surprising about such behaviour in East Germany), he answered that an author does not need to be a 'moral model . . . Goethe was a swine, so was Brecht. Why not me?'

The business of justice is full of injustices. That is the problem we face when we go seeking to find it. Why is it that those with overall responsibility for acts of torture and genocide should be judged, while the people who did the killing, torturing and dismembering of their fellow humans are exempted from punishment? Wouldn't it be better if the people who carried out the crimes in practice and committed atrocities with the clear conscience of those who are 'only following orders' were made an example of? Since it is obviously impossible to bring everybody to court, it is perhaps more practical to make choices. But even these choices will always be open to challenge. An analogy that makes me uneasy with myself comes to mind. Whenever I do the shopping for a meal that has meat in it, I buy pre-packed meat in a package that has no obvious relation with the animal that was slaughtered for that purpose. I can never buy meat at a butcher's without feeling sick at the sight of parts of dead animals, let alone the sight of a whole slaughtered sheep or chicken. I know that I am acting as a hypocrite, as if the act was not committed just because it was not committed before my eyes. This hypocrite has no right to pretend to be more sensitive than others.

The business of legal justice in a plural society is not an easy matter. In a totalitarian society, it is not even in the running; it is at best a parody. Judith N. Shklar [*Legalism: Law,*

Morals and Political Trials, Harvard University Press, Cambridge, Massachusetts, 1986] does a fascinating job in showing how difficult it is to combine justice, morality and politics, and how decency can be faced with difficult choices:

> For a social action to be termed just, however, one must first agree that it is in conformity with one's system of rules, and since in any conceivable modern society there are always several competing systems of rules, it is not possible to say that any rule or act as such is just. [. . .] Justice has been called a 'quasi-morality' because it is not a virtue that is always relevant or valued. In personal relations it has not always been rated very highly.

Shklar deals at length with the enormous legacy of Nazi horrors. The Nuremberg trials still provide a rich source for thought on this matter. But lately we have been submerged with other cases of crimes against humanity, war crimes and horrible massacres arising out of ethnic conflicts.

> In the last five years, just at the point where we are about to say farewell to the twentieth century, there have been ninety armed conflicts in the world, which have combined to create a population of 20 million refugees. Only four of these conflicts have been wars between states. The other eighty-six have been wars of hatred between peoples. Civil, ethnic and tribal conflicts. And they have not happened only in the 'Third World'. [See Flora Lewis, *International Herald Tribune*, 5 May 1995]

In the course of 1996–7 we had the misfortune of having to witness on our TV screens and in our daily papers a series of horrible massacres. For me, watching became a nightmarish exercise in facing up to my own memories. The experience of Lebanon was repeating itself in countries as far removed as Rwanda and ex-Yugoslavia. The difference lied not in the faces and the looks of the people that I saw on TV. The Serb, Croatian and Bosnian fighters could have been carbon copies of the Lebanese militias; they held their rifles and their cigarettes in the same way that Said held his; they relaxed after combat with the same nonchalance as that of Latifa and her comrades in their headquarters; they had a similar way of suddenly getting up and going forward on some dubious task or mission. The eyes of the Rwandan refugees also showed the same anguish as those of Lebanese families hiding in the shelter of their buildings, or of a driver showing his identity card at a checkpoint composed of militia from the opposite religious sect. The difference was not there. It lay rather in the concern with justice and retribution. and the means that the international or local communities were proposing in order to deal with these situations.

Two recent cases serve to sow confusion: the case of Dusko Tadik, a Serb from Bosnia who appeared before the International Court of Justice at the Hague, accused of war crimes; and that of Ngoyambe, a 17-year-old youth and one of the first Rwandans to be brought before the Kigali tribunal set up to judge those responsible for the genocide.

At the time of his trial, Dusko Tadic was 39 years old. He had been named as the executioner at the Omarska camp in the north-west of Bosnia, where Bosnian prisoners were kept. He was recognized by some of his surviving victims while visiting his brother in Germany. He was caught and charged with war crimes, complicity in genocide, murder and rape. He was brought before the International Court of Justice at the Hague, to be judged by a tribunal that had been created in 1993 by a resolution of the UN Security Council. The tribunal's task was to judge the crimes that had been committed in ex-Yugoslavia, along the lines of the Nuremberg trials. The things that Tadic was accused of were so horrific that I could not bring myself to read the description of his alleged tortures, and the savage humiliations that he imposed on his prisoners and forced them to do to others. The descriptions made me sick.

The point is that in the same issue of *Le Monde* newspaper, 28 April 1995, there were three articles analysing and describing the case of Tadic. Three journalists who had thought over the problem could not agree, though, on the benefits, rights or merits of such a trial. The editorial of *Le Monde* that day called this trial the alibi of the hypocrites. It indicated the incongruous analogy with the Nuremberg Trials:

As an excuse for the level of modesty of the case, La Haye's authorities for this case said that they will cite as suspects Radovan Karadzick, the chief of the Bosnian Serbs, as well as General Ratko Mladic, the commander of his army.

'Is it enough to give public opinion the illusion that justice will be done for war crimes in Bosnia?' asks the editor. The column concludes with an angry tone that this tribunal is inventing something ridiculous in order to hide its total impotence and passivity towards 'ethnic cleansing'.

This is not exactly the same attitude expressed by Pierre Georges, on top of the back page of the same issue of *Le Monde*, who writes despising the likes of Tadic: 'History is full of these non-guilty executioners, assassins. Current events too.' None the less, Georges too is not at ease with 'Judging instead of preventing because one cannot do better . . . The world according to Tadic is not afraid of these judges.'

Neither is the world according to Ngoyambe, the Hutu teenager waiting to be judged in Kigali, where he faces accusations of six murders and a charge of genocide. His reaction? He is not afraid of judges as such. In his opinion: 'The only danger is if the judge is Tutsi . . . If he is Hutu, there will be no judicial error.'

At the time when Ngoyame was speaking, 32,000 other prisoners were crammed into Rwanda's prison and detention centres, also under the accusation of genocide. Among them were hundreds of children under 14 years of age, whom UNICEF was attempting to have transferred to juvenile centres.

To the reasonable question of what 'judgement' might mean in such circumstances, the answer of Rene Degni Segui, rector of the Faculty of Law in Abidjan and founding president of the Ivory Coast League of Human Rights, is pertinent: 'We have to break with the African tradition of impunity. In Rwanda and in Burundi there had been many previous waves of massacres. The Prefects and the Town Chiefs responsible for these massacres have been allowed to stay in their positions. Sometimes they have been rewarded.' Segui is in favour of bringing the culprits to trial, for he believes in the preventive and dissuasive role of judgement for future occasions, and in neighbouring countries. His fear is that 'The immediate causes of the genocide – the refusal of alternation and incitement to ethnic hatred – are in bud in all African states.' [*Le Monde*, 6 April 1995]

Young Ngoyame and the not-so-young Tadic both claim their innocence. They were following orders. The same difficult old story, again and again. They all were and are performing their duties. Hannah Arendt repeats a dialogue recorded by an American journalist in November 1944, and calls it a work worthy of a great poet:

Q: Did you kill people in the camp?

A: Yes.

Q: Did you poison them with gas?

A: Yes.

Q: Did you bury them alive?

A: It sometimes happened.

Q: Were the victims picked from all over Europe?

A: I suppose so.

Q: Did you personally help kill people?

A: Absolutely not, I was only paymaster in the camp.

Q: What did you think of what was going on?

A: It was bad at first but we got used to it.

Q: Do you know the Russians will hang you?

A: (Bursting into tears) Why should they? What have I done?

The paymaster meant that he was following orders, no more, no less. I don't know whether he is lying to himself, or whether he is being absurdly sincere. A sincerity like that of Ngoyambe, who is in a way incapable of guilt, for the world according to him is divided into only two spheres, that of the Hutus and that of the Tutsis. In his opinion, any punishment would be very unfair indeed.

The responsibility or the innocence of those who 'simply followed orders' is the most difficult to assess, and thus to judge. From Eichmann and Rudolf Hess to Tadic and Ngoyambe, and most probably to the men who blinded Iraq's children in order to instil fear into their parents, we hear repeatedly, whether in good or bad faith, that they had no choice ... that they were following orders ... that they could not be held responsible ... and thus should not be punished. Up to now the only argument that could be raised against those who 'simply followed orders' has been that some, a few, a tiny minority chose *not* to follow orders.

Here it is worth remembering the case which Günter Grass has raised (see the exchange of letters between Günter Grass and Kinzaburo Oe in *The Guardian*, 6 May 1995) – that of the deserters from the German armed forces during the Nazi period – which unfortunately aroused much less attention than that of the killers of that period. According to Grass, 20,000 Germans were court-marshalled and sentenced to death. They were hanged in the most brutal ways possible, and exposed in public with signs on their bodies saying: 'I am a coward'. The hanging streets were called 'Hitler's alleys' for the occasion. These 'real heroes of the war', as Grass sees them, are still filed as cowards and deserters. They are the ones who refused to follow orders. Do they not deserve rehabilitation and justice at least as urgently and as publicly as those who gave the orders that they refused to obey? Or are people less concerned because of some nationalist streak in the victors' camp, whereby we hide behind the 'collective responsibility of the Germans' rather than opting to look into this dark grey area of the human beings that we are – the human beings that Primo Levi explores with such painful lucidity?

Primo Levi, who did not always pardon but who worked very hard to be 'free of the vice of hatred', insists on the distinction between those who inspired, held power and initiated and those who were their victims and acted as executioners for them. He describes at length and in frightening detail the horrific 'social organization' of the concentration camps, a 'totalitarian' mini-society of slavery and death, in which the victims were forced by the German administration to participate in the torture and killing of other inmates. Levi speaks with dark words of a grey area, the space that separates the persecutors in the Nazi camps from their victims. This area, he says, is never empty:

It never is; it is studded with obscene and pathetic figures (sometimes they possess both qualities simultaneously), whom it is essential to know if we want to know the human species, if we want to know how to defend our souls when a similar test once more looms before us.

Levi speaks about (and for) those prisoners who were chosen

by the Nazi concentration camp administrators to run the gas chambers and the crematoria. He speaks of them as victims, who were already too destroyed psychologically and physically to have shown any resistance. Often they performed their deathly duties without creating problems. But we should remember that not all accepted. There were exceptions. Levi tells of a group of 400 Jewish prisoners from Corfu who rebelled and refused to perform tasks that would have turned them into the executioners of other inmates. They were immediately gassed, all of them.

> It is necessary, however, to declare that before such human cases it is imprudent to hasten to issue a moral judgement. It must be clear that the greatest responsibility lies with the system, the very structure of the totalitarian state, the concurrent guilt on the part of the individual collaborators, both large and small.

Levi is all the more tortured by the knowledge that the fact of being a victim in such totalitarian situations does not exclude culpability. In *Republic of Fear*, Samir al-Khalil describes a similar situation – the attempt, often successful, by Saddam Hussein's totalitarian regime in Iraq to turn normal, decent people into collaborators with the crimes of the dictatorship.

Who among us can answer honestly how they would resist if they had to face what some of Saddam's victims had to face: a man's wife tortured and raped before his eyes . . . the torture and blinding of his children . . . Who can say that they would refuse the order to commit atrocities in the face of such things?

There is very little place for humanity in these inhuman settings, and when people claim that it was difficult as jailers and executioners, in the Argentinian army, or in the concentration camps, 'at the beginning . . . but we got used to it' they are not lying. They are not even finding excuses. They are merely describing a reality that has been all too common.

Remember Hannah Arendt's reply to Germans who said that, after what happened in the thirties and forties, they were ashamed of being German: 'I have often felt tempted to answer that I am ashamed of being human.' [Hannah Arendt, 'Organised guilt and universal responsibility' in Smith, R.W., ed. *Guilt: Man and Society*, Anchor Books, New York, 1971] Many centuries before, the great Arab poet al-Mutanabbi had written bitter verses deploring this same human condition:

I am doubting the one I chose
for I know he belongs to the human race.

Arendt comes close to Levi's belief that the persecutors engulf their victims in their crimes when she says – one is tempted to say almost cynically – that 'German refugees, who had the good fortune either to be Jews, or have been persecuted by the Gestapo early enough, have been saved from the guilt is of course not their merit. Because they know this and because their horror at what might have been still haunts them, they often introduce into discussions of this kind that insufferable tone of self-righteousness which frequently and particularly among Jews, can turn into the vulgar obverse of Nazi doctrines, and in fact already has.' *ibid*. One wonders whether Arendt is concerned more with compassion for the guilty than with the judgement of the self-righteous.

That woman who was frantically assaulting that prisoner with the hammer, and who still haunts my horrified memory, had no sense that she was guilty of anything. In that civil war, as in all other civil wars, the areas of neutral space in which our daily life as human beings is ordinarily lived was reduced to almost nil. People struggled to maintain that space of neutrality in the corridors of their homes, turning them into shelters into which they piled anything that might remind them of civilizat'on while at the same time caring for others.

The woman with the hammer had lost contact with normal reality. The people who tried to calm her down could not decide whether she was mad, or whether she was simply doing on an individual basis what was done routinely every time an 'enemy camp' was seized. I find myself wondering whether a similar number of people would have tried to stop the madness if the person holding the hammer had been a male.

If the greater responsibility lies with the system, as Primo Levi says, then why not judge the system and leave the people to deal with their guilt on their own? Tempting as it may be, such a statement really makes no sense. It is obvious that in almost all cases of crime, be they war crimes, private crimes, or crimes against humanity, something has to be done.

The conclusion of the 1989 conference organized by the Aspen Institute on 'State Crimes, Punishment or Pardon' was forthright:

Although there were different views as to the extent of the

obligation to punish, there was common agreement that the successor government has an obligation to investigate and establish the facts so that the truth be known and be made part of the nation's history. Even in situations where pardon or clemency might be appropriate, there should be no compromising of the obligation to discover and acknowledge the truth ... The identity of the victims and what happened to them, and the identity of the planners and of the perpetrators must be made known ... Truth telling, it was agreed, responds to the demand of justice for the victims ...

This might be a possible response to situations such as those in Latin America and the rule of military dictatorships. As one of the participants in this conference observed:

Where a society has been fractured by a tyrannical regime and must be reconstructed and repaired, it may be a reasonable assumption, in some cases, that a degree of pacification will achieve more for human rights, in the long run, than insisting on punishment and risking political instability and continued social divisiveness.

Forgiving and Judging

Mario Vargas Llosa expressed a similar idea in an article entitled 'Playing with Fire' (*Le Monde*, 18 May 1995), in which he called for forgiveness in Argentina:

Judging and punishing all the extraordinary cruelties perpetrated in Argentina? It would be wonderful, but it is impossible in practical terms ... [The Argentinians] should get over their nausea – which is understandable – and their horror, and look towards countries such as Spain and Chile that have found ways of breaking the vicious circle, and have succeeded in burying the past in order to build a future. It is only when democracy has taken root, and a culture of legality and freedom has impregnated the whole society, that a country can be said to have armed itself against bestial violence ...

These lines triggered a series of angry responses from writers and lawyers that were printed in *Le Monde* a week later. Llosa was spared no insult on those pages. Accusations of bad faith, ignorance, and cowardice, and even of advancing arguments that simply rephrased the Junta's own justifications.

The conference at the Aspen Institute and the debate between Llosa and his critics were not dealing with situations of ethnic cleansing on the scale of the Holocaust or the massacre of the Armenians at the turn of the century. Nor were they dealing with the atrocities committed in Lebanon, Yugoslavia, Rwanda and elsewhere. They did not consider the responsibility of the victims when the choice was not between good and evil but 'between murder and murder'. Their concern was: how can one be just and call for the exercise of justice, not for the sake of avenging the past, but for the sake of less future suffering? This question is not becoming easier in our modern world. On the one hand, 'Even good and, at bottom, worthy people have, in our time, the most extraordinary fear about making judgements' (Arendt, *ibid*, p.338). On the other, according to Shklar, who is trying to achieve the impossible task of demarcating the political from the legal in this domain, it is precisely because of our modernity that the task is becoming less easy: 'For a social action to be termed just, however, one must first agree that it is in conformity with one's system of rules, and since in any conceivable modern society there are always several competing systems of rules, it is not possible to say that any rule as such is just.'

Let us take an example: in Lebanon a system of rules based on the rights of the individual co-exists side by side with recognition of rules of tribal and blood relations. This fact accounts for the lenient punishments handed out in so-called 'crimes of honour'.

[I remember, as a teenager, having read the frightening story of a man who had failed in his attempt to kill his daughter, who had been found not to be a virgin before her marriage. During the course of his one-year jail sentence for this attempt, he heard that his son had succeeded in murdering the poor woman. His reaction was complete jubilation. He started dancing and singing in jail. In a similar case of coexistence of differing systems of rules and contradictions, we might look at the judge who freed the Turkish mother and father in Paris, who had killed their daughter in order to preserve the honour of the family, and the angry reactions of feminist and individual human rights organisations. Postmodernism, unsurprisingly, did not produce many texts in the area of legislation!]

But Shklar is aware that political trials are not like ordinary criminal cases in their determination of legality and justice. This is because political interests, actions and circumstances, and people's attitudes towards them are constantly in a process of change and are subject to conflicts of opinion. This is why Shklar observes, convincingly, that the main value of the Nuremberg Trials lies in the historical facts that they unearthed about Nazi government. [One should remember that these trials put Germany's war criminals and ethnic cleansing policies in the dock, but never thought to try the war crimes for which some Allied commanders had been responsibile.]

> The Nuremberg Trail of 1945 was not remarkable only because it was something entirely new in the history of international law. It was a great drama in which the most fundamental moral and political values were the real personae. Emotionally and philosophically it confronted every thoughtful individual with the necessity of making some clear decision about his beliefs.

Reconciliation

In Lebanon, in 1994, the victims of a massacre in the Chouf area were invited to participate in a three-day conference on 'Acknowledgement, Forgiveness and Reconciliation – Alternative approaches to conflict resolution in Lebanon' (the proceedings were later published by University College, Beirut, April 1994). The village concerned, Maasir al-Chouf, a Christian enclave in a Druze dominated area, had lived in peace for the major part of the civil war. So much so that a few days before the massacre, a number of French journalists, invited to visit this haven of civil war coexistence between two rival communities, had rushed home to write articles under headlines such as 'Peace is still possible in Lebanon', illustrated with big pictures of the local priest and the Druze sheikh shaking hands and smiling. The journalists wrote their articles on 7 March 1977. On 16 March, following the death of Kemal Jumblatt, Druze armed men opened fire on Christian houses in Maasir al-Chouf. They also kidnapped Christians in the village and killed them. When those self-same journalists – who felt betrayed – asked if they could visit the village again, officials of Jumblatt's PSP (Parti Socialiste Populaire) told them that they could visit Maasir al-Chouf if they first visited Kfar Matta, a village where the Christian militias had massacred Druze inhabitants.

In this conference for reconciliation, designed to encourage the relocation of the Christian refugees in their village of Maasir, the victims of the violence made a statement. 'We buried our dead with dignity, we transcended our wounds and we forgave ... The State wants time to work towards a solution; time would weaken resentment, and the effect of forgetting would be that the demands for justice would recede. We, the victims, are not asking for the impossible. But we refuse to be ignored, neglected and subjected to a *fait accompli*. We insist on our right to return to our village and our land. This is why we find it necessary to enter into a process of dialogue based on reflection and compensation, and to create acceptable solutions so that we do not turn the future into a field of experimentation for human brotherhood, which has no guarantee of success ... We believe in giving back pride to its owners . . . at the same time we believe in the logic of coexistence.'

There is something tragic in these words. Tragic not only in the rhetorical tone that the victims felt that they had to adopt in the context of a semi-official conference, but also in the genuine inner struggle of these people – their need for justice, which they are trying to minimize, and their fear for the future if nothing ends up being said about responsibility for the massacres. There is a dignity here, despite the tone of Arabic rhetoric, similar to the dignity with which they had buried their dead.

If the need for vengeance is a fact of life, the meaning of civilized coexistence has long been rightly understood as the intervention by legal or social procedures in order to limit the possibility of this vengeance, and to use legal means and compensations in order to re-establish a possible coexistence between the one who did the injury and the person injured. But the advanced Western societies are themselves not immune to outbursts of barbarism. I still cannot believe that a Home Secretary of the British government, Michael Howard, could promise in a BBC radio interview that any decision on the length of a sentence of imprisonment would take into account the way the public viewed the possible release of the prisoners. He was addressing the case of the two young boys who had murdered the three-year-old James Bulger. When it appeared after the court hearings that the child murderers might be freed after eight or ten years, the parents of the victim, as well as a large part of the public, were full of grief and anger. In one phrase the Home Secretary threw away one of the pillars of law-based societies: to take the business of punishment out of the hands of the victims and out of the hands of those members of society who may see themselves as possible future victims. As Neal Ascherson commented in an indignant article in *The Independent* (30 January 1994) entitled 'When punishment becomes revenge, we're on the road to barbarism': 'The doctrine of retribution, the infliction of pain to ease pain, is shambling back, a tattered ghost which once seemed to have been laid for good ... But what matters is to understand what a leap backwards this [Howard's declaration] is. As soon as it occurred to our ancestors that government might be about happiness rather than obedience, it was seen that punishment under the law must be designed to achieve something good, rather than balance something evil.' Yes, the 'civilized countries' are not immune.

Barbaric ideas need to be exposed, but unfortunately such ideas are often put into practice. Being myself against the death penalty, I cannot agree with the conclusion of Arendt, who after a lucid exposition of these matters joins the opinion that since Eichmann did not want to share this earth with the Jewish people and the people of other nations, 'we find that no one, that is, no member of the human race, can be expected to want to share the earth with you. This is the reason, and the only reason, you must hang.'

Arendt is a very political person. I would prefer to leave the last word – not in the sense of a conclusion, but as another question mark – to Bertold Brecht, to the language of tragicomedy:

The great political criminals must be exposed, and exposed especially to laughter. They are not great political criminals, but people who permitted great political crimes, which is something entirely different . . . One may say that tragedy deals with the suffering of mankind in a less serious way than comedy. [Brecht's notes for *The Irresistible Rise of Arturo Ui*, cited by Hannah Arendt in *Men in Dark Times*]